ROSE'S KISS

❀

The Legacy of Rhoslefain, ABBEY CHRONICLES I

Joy Ann Harber

iUniverse, Inc.

New York Lincoln Shanghai

Rose's Kiss
The Legacy of Rhoslefain, ABBEY CHRONICLES I

All Rights Reserved © 2003 by Joy Ann Harber

No part of this book may be reproduced or transmitted in any form or by any means, graphic, electronic, or mechanical, including photocopying, recording, taping, or by any information storage retrieval system, without the written permission of the publisher.

iUniverse, Inc.

For information address:
iUniverse, Inc.
2021 Pine Lake Road, Suite 100
Lincoln, NE 68512
www.iuniverse.com

ISBN: 0-595-27425-0

Printed in the United States of America

For Roger, after all these years together, you still take my breath away.
You'll forever be my Knight.
I love you.

Contents

❀

ACKNOWLEDGMENTS...

First and foremost I wish to thank the God of all creation, for giving me this story. To Him alone be all praise and glory. Bidden or unbidden, God is here.

I cannot begin to list the number of people who have encouraged me to write this book.

I wish to thank them all, especially Will Essex and Daniel McDowell for sharing such creative ideas, and for bringing out the best in me as a writer. You challenged me to dig deeper and embrace the darker threads of the tapestry. To Sarah Bussard and Tami Robbins, for your undying support and encouragement, and to the gang at the Roann Public Library, in Roann Indiana, for believing in me. To my husband, Roger and our children, Patrick and Shelby, I thank you for letting me be myself, however crazy that may be. I thank you all so much.

—Joy Harber

PROLOGUE

❀

Avril 1309
Southern Border,
Realm of Dundrennan, Britain

Billows of acrid, black smoke drifted from the blood-soaked fields. The putrid smell of burnt hair and charred bodies hung heavily in the late afternoon air. Wild cries from over the hills were met with the ringing clang of steel. Blade against blade; the clash was spectacular. It was dangerously beautiful like lightning on a summer's eve.

Marauders from across the North Sea sought to take the land of Britain; specifically Dundrennan. In defense, Ruffian and his men fought on. Those from Sedgemoor, and all points beyond, moved together in fearsome unison. Like a grandly choreographed dance, they advanced together; ever forward, no retreat.

His men died around him. Their horses screamed; eyes wild with fear at the melee that surrounded them. The smoke was stinging his eyes, as Ruffian looked to the hills.

"Where are our damnable support troops? They were due here two days hence! Aye, 'Tis easy enough for the Crown to involve us in such a fight but where are the men he promised us? I daresay it costs Edward II little or nothing to send us out here to die. Do our lives mean so little, Ethan?" he spat out between blows.

"Our spotters say two thousand dead," Ethan Bardougne called out.

"Our men?"

"Theirs, m'lord."

How many had he killed himself that day alone? Brave young lads with as much sense of duty as he? He'd lost count. Ruffian had the ability to disassociate himself from the carnage of battle. Like a machine, he carried out the objectives without dwelling on the ramifications of the lives he was ending.

At that moment, he instinctively whirled around and buried his broadsword into the chest of yet one more.

"M'lord?" the young man yelped as he looked into Ruffian's eyes. He couldn't have been more than 18 summers old. His green eyes grew wide in shock before starring forevermore unseeing into the early evening sky.

"God, what have I done?" Ruffian gasped. Ethan had seen what happened and rode quickly to Ruffian's side.

"He's one of ours."

"Nay! He can't be! He was coming at me!" Ruffian screamed.

"'Tis getting dark; perhaps he didn't recognize you from behind. The boy was young and inexperienced," Ethan reasoned.

"Do you know his name?"

"Callum Lindsey. I think his family is from Breckonshire," Ethan called over his shoulder as he rushed to help another man from Sedgemoor. It was common to lose good men in battle. War was like that. But Ruffian held a different view. Especially when one died by his hand. Each life caused a ripple effect upon so many others. He knelt over the boy and withdrew his blade. A whisper of steam escaped the wound and drifted away into the night. He tenderly closed the green eyes with a shaking hand.

"I am so sorry," he whispered.

Before he could stand, he felt the moment of impact. Steel meeting bone, and bone yielding to its adversary. Looking down, Ruffian saw the tip of a sword protruding from his left shoulder. He held his breath as the warrior savagely withdrew his blade, making a soft hissing sound. He felt a sickening vibration as the ragged edge of his broken shoulder blade grated across the retreating steel. A comrade from Sedgemoor ended the warrior's life immediately afterward.

The fire spread quickly down Ruffian's left arm and across his chest. The front of his tunic and chain mail was slick with blood. It pumped out steadily with every heartbeat.

"Oh God, save me," he moaned, "I can't die tonight." He staggered to the edge of the tree line and fell to the ground. He rolled onto his back and tried to slow his breathing and pulse. The trees towered above him, surrounding him. They swayed gently in the breeze. The fluid motion calmed him. He could hear Ethan calling for him, but he could no longer respond. Already, he saw the tiny pin pricks of light dance before his eyes. The trees gently faded from view.

The drummers and pipers played on in the distance. Silver threads of a melody floated faintly on the air. The tune took him back home, to a time when all was safe and well. Children laughed and squealed as they chased each other around the creamery at Sedgemoor. There was no smoke, and the sunlight felt warm and welcoming upon his face. He closed his eyes and savored it all.

The shouts and cries of battle faded from his consciousness; replaced by the soft sweet crooning of a tune. Ruffian felt a gentle hand stroking his brow. A strange sort of peace came as darkness finally overtook him. He swore he heard a voice calling his name from far away. For where your treasure is, there your heart is also.

The journey had begun…

CHAPTER 1

❀

AND LOVE WILL LEAD HIM HOME

Mai 1309
Sedgemoor

It was before dawn when Ruffian and Ethan finally reached Sedgemoor territory. Ruffian's saddle softly creaked in rhythm with Thunder's relaxed gait. They reached the cliffs atop the brooding Tywynn Sea just before the sunrise. Leaving Ethan to his rest, Ruffian stepped to the uneven edge of rock; as far as he dared. Stunning blue conifers surrounded the spot that gave way to the vast vista of the churning sea below, a wash of green and blue.

"Lord, here I am. On the very edge of the world. On the edge of my life. It's only you and me here now. What is the plan? You could've ended things a few weeks ago, but you didn't. Am I to assume there's something more for me here?" he kicked a few loose pebbles off the edge of the cliff.

"Have I been gone too long? Lord, you know my heart. You know what I want. If that be your plan for me, I'd pray you'd make it so." Ruffian stepped over to a huge boulder and climbed atop it. He closed his eyes and breathed in the fresh sea air. It cleansed him from the stench of death. He pulled out his tattered journal, the one thing his mother had gifted him with before he left, and began to inscribe his thoughts.

How long has it been since I last saw her face? I know 'twas just months ago, but alas it seems a lifetime has passed since then. Do the feelings still live within her? I wonder. I guess I shall see if time and distance has changed things. She seemed so far away, yet somehow I felt her near me that night. Gracing the steps to Heaven, 'twas her I'm sure that brought me back. What a curious thing, this time and space we live in.

Has time made us distant? Tessa and I? The miles were but rippled shadows of a fleeting fear; an illusion brought to light by the knowledge of something better. The time is but the smallest twitch of a blink. Nay, distant is not my word. "Genuine" would be the description of my choosing.

I still carry the aroma of the woods and meadows in my mind. The muskiness of that black cloak will never set me free, Lord willing. Not to mention the look on her face as we teased each other like children at the edge of the misty ponds. She will remember as I do. One touch and it will be as if I never left.

"Are we ready to ride, Ruffian?" Ethan asked, rubbing his stiff neck and offering his brother the last drop of water from his skins. The sun arose over the cliffs as if the Eternal One had heard his earnest plea. The castle, Sedgemoor, awakened from its misty shroud and gleamed in the dawn's soft light. Ruffian wondered at the name of that pinkish orange colour that washed over the morning sky. It was one of those treasures he would tuck away, for no words could ever do it justice.

It had been over six months since they'd left Sedgemoor's gates to serve both Laird and Crown. They'd defended the coast, and Ruffian had led his men bravely. He returned wounded; but alive, and well compensated for his efforts. Gold, he found, served nicely to ease his conscious. Though sometimes he could still see those scared green eyes looking back at him amid the haze of his dreams.

Ruffian directed Thunder down the steep forest path that led to Sedgemoor's gates. He reveled in the aromas of earth; trying to dispel the smoke from his lungs once and for all. Ancient trees arose around him, bearing the mark of time. Sedgemoor lay tucked away in the countryside of Dundrennan. It was a region of Britain that would in the future be called by another name. However, travelers had always sensed an energy or life force there, no matter what the land was called.

Streaming garlands of roses and ivy draped themselves seductively over the stone walls of Sedgemoor's outer keep. Their perfume enticed the morning air. Of course, the villagers were already up and about their day. From a distance, he heard a door shut a dog bark. As Ruffian and Ethan approached, the gates were opened. *All hail, the conquering hero,* he thought. They both just wanted a hot bath, a warm bed and a meal that was truly edible.

"I'm not at all sure just what we lived on those last few days of the campaign," Ruffian mumbled.

"Some sort of gray meat...*with sauce,*" Ethan said. A shudder ran through both of them at the memory of it.

They entered the bailey to the cheers of the people. Ethan was swallowed up in the gathering crowd. Ruffian glanced up to the tower as he tossed his reins to the groomsman. He spied her immediately. She stood in the doorway of her chamber balcony, half-hidden in the shadows. He watched as she disappeared.

Just then, a firm but loving hand touched his shoulder. Jolie Bardougne looked into the face of her eldest son. She had tried to place both he and Ethan in God's hands when the battle had first begun. But the weeks had turned to months with no word, and sometimes a mother's prayers turn to pleading deep in the night.

"M'lady, I have surely missed the light in your eyes." He kissed her on the forehead.

"You are well?" she asked as she studied him closer.

"Aye, Lady, nothing ails me that some food and good company won't cure." He pulled the woman to him. She became his mother at age 16 and the two had nearly grown up together. Still, the petite woman in his arms was the anchor in his life. Clinging just as fiercely to him, she closed her eyes and whispered her thanks to the heavens.

They parted reluctantly, as Jolie knew she must share him just now, with the Laird of Sedgemoor. She stepped back and watched her son make his way to the keep. A bittersweet smile played upon her lips. For it had always been that way. She had always shared him with the MacLures.

Ruffian took the worn stone steps two at a time as he headed toward the great hall. Laird MacLure and his family would be gathering soon to break their fast. Tessa saw him arrive. She'd be there soon, he knew she would. As he reached the landing, she was waiting for him. Contessa Faith MacLure, she was the object of his obsession. She wanted to throw her arms around his neck and never let go. *Or maybe just my hands around his neck would suffice*, she thought.

"I see you are not dead in some peat bog," she casually said, "Six months with no word, what was I to think?"

"Um, there wasn't exactly daily missive service. We were a little busy down there, you know, preserving life as you know it, and all," he ground out through clenched teeth.

Tessa looked past him to the view of the horizon through the tall arched window and sighed. He was her confidante, her 'truefriend'. There was an unspoken bond forged so early in their childhood that neither had any recollection of its birth. She wanted badly just to slap him, instead she reached up and lightly traced a finger across his left shoulder. He looked to see tears glittering in her warm brown eyes. He took her trembling hand within his own, and turning it over, he ever so softly kissed her palm.

"I'm all right, Tessa, its healing just fine," he whispered, "I'm thankful Artemis sent those herbs along with Ethan." Tessa laughed out loud, "Aye, let's not forget that weeds are our friends!"

Of course she had known the moment it had happened. She'd been on edge all that evening. Her parents had been entertaining friends for dinner, but Tessa was in no mood for food or covert conversation about the latest scandals at court. As the lute and lyre were being played, she excused herself and nimbly slipped from the keep via the tunnel that lay just beyond the knight's garrison. She followed the moon to the cliffs of the Tywynn Sea.

The moon was high in the clouds, but no stars dared twinkle that night. She knew something was amiss with Ruffian; she could feel it in her spirit. The wind was rising from off the sea. Its tangy spray stung her face. Tessa stood there alone in the night. She begged the 'Powers That Be' to bring him home alive. She reached up to the heavens beyond, her dark woolen cloak billowing out behind her. A jagged bolt of deep blue lightning danced across the sky. It was at that moment Tessa screamed into the howling wind and fell to the ground. Nearly an hour later she stirred.

How long have I been here? she wondered, as she gathered her senses. Something had happened. Was she dead? Was he? No, she felt he yet breathed. He was hurt; she knew, perhaps mortally, out there somewhere in the night.

He gently squeezed her hand, bringing her back to the present. He saw all the emotions play across her face as she remembered. A tear ran down her cheek and dropped upon his boot. He grinned as he brushed the rest away with his callused thumbs.

"I think I heard your voice that night, Tessa, you sounded so far away, but it was the thought of you that brought me back. See now, m'lady, I stand before you *almost* fully intact. You needn't fear, for I'll not leave unless requested to do so. Now, may we eat?"

"My boy! How good it is to have you back home. Come and eat!" Tormond MacLure called. Tormond Alisdare MacLure was an imposing figure of a man. He was indeed a savage warrior, most honored knight of the realm, and the beloved Laird to all at Sedgemoor. He was known to be both merciful and merciless. It was much better to be within his good graces than outside them. He was a huge man; tall and muscular. Deep auburn hair curled down to his fur-trimmed collar. The gray had just begun to lightly kiss his beard and temples. No one in the land would dare disobey him; except the wench across the table who happened to be his daughter.

"By the heavens, you look half-starved!" Elspeth cried when she saw Ruffian step into the hall. Tormond's wife fussed and fretted over Ruffian; fixing his plate, as if he were still six years old. He shook his head and laughed to himself. Tessa just rolled her eyes; she couldn't remember her mother ever fixing her plate.

"What would my fellow soldiers say if they could see me now?"

"I daresay they'd envy your plate filled to overflowing with roasted pigeon and cheese with brandied pears and fresh barley bread, young man!" Elspeth said in the 'tone' that Ruffian knew so well. She had a way of putting the most fiercesome warrior in his place.

Ruffian couldn't remember life before Sedgemoor. They said he came to foster at age four. It was a common practice of the day. He never remembered leaving his own parents. He lived with Jolie and Rod Bardougne, the weaver and stable master of the keep. Ethan, their son, was just a year younger than Ruffian, and they were all shocked when several years later, little Serrah came along. He remembered Tormond's massive hands on his thin shoulders when he broke the news of his parent's deaths. He was assured he'd always have a home at Sedgemoor. Having nowhere to go after earning his silver spurs, Tormond invited Ruffian to stay.

"I'm not about to have a well-trained knight gallivant across the countryside and defend another man's keep!" Tormond had a way of making everything sound as if he was only looking out after his own interests. Ruffian knew better.

They ate and laughed and talked till he thought he'd fall asleep right in his brandied pears. He was exhausted, but he hated for the moment to end. Mundane talk of the price of spices and the last batch of bad goat cheese was a healing balm to a warrior's battered heart. From across the table, Tessa felt his eyes upon her. Scared to look back, she was compelled to. Ruffian lifted his tankard and drank deeply of his wine. His eyes never left hers. He grinned. She nearly choked on a piece of pigeon and looked away.

"Ah, I see the dance has begun, my dear," Elspeth whispered into her husband's ear as she placed a gentle kiss there.

CHAPTER 2

❀

RHOSLEFAIN ABBEY

Within the dream of fanciful flight, she could hear the music calling her. Far away, it seemed, subdued by the veil of sleep. As she made her way through the forest flowers and down the winding path leading back to conscious thought, she followed the melody home. Awakening in her darkened chamber; a dying peat fire her only light, Tessa walked to her tower window. Wisps of perfumed breezes beckoned her onto her stone balcony. Her gauzy gown flowed gracefully around her in the night air.

From where she stood, she could see Rhoslefain Abbey, *the Abbey of Roses.* It was a curiously enchanted place. Travelers assumed the abbey was in ruins, what with no roof and only partial walls that were now grown over with brambles and flowering vines. Looking closer, the abbey told a different tale. The high, arched, iron gate opened unto a sanctuary of energy, emotion and spirituality.

A marble floor, inlaid with an elaborate prayer labyrinth made of quartz was still visible under the deep green moss and wandering thyme that grew within the cracks of the stone itself. Crafted by artisans before the time of anyone's recollection, it was a known fact that the castle Sedgemoor had been built on earlier ruins of some sort of religious order. However, Rhoslefain Abbey was no ruin. It simply had never been finished. Though there were plenty of legends and lore about why construction on the abbey had been stopped, no one knew for sure what happened to those inhabitants of Rhoslefain over a century before. Tangled vines of ivy climbed the abbey walls, as nature slowly reclaimed the spot for herself. Later years had brought the addition of roses and boxwood as the abbey was transformed into an intricate garden maze for the amusement of Sedgemoor's guests.

It had always been Tessa's favorite place. Truly a sanctuary, she spent her childhood playing there. She knew every secret passageway, every short cut, and dead end. Something drew her there. Many hours were spent within the gentle protection of the abbey's walls. Tracing the labyrinth, she did her best soul-searching there. At the center of the labyrinth was an altar of sorts, a place to surrender all to God. Almost like a vibrating hum, Tessa felt an indescribable sense of energy there. The music from her dreamed played on and seemed to be coming from the heart of the maze.

Slipping from the castle via the usual tunnel, Tessa cautiously approached the abbey gate. She feared the old iron gate would creak in protest but it gave way with only a slight push. Hesitantly, she entered her sanctuary. It looked much different at night. The tiny reflecting ponds mirrored the blue moon that graced the sky. She heard whispers in the trees around her. Singing, laughing; the night had come alive.

Tessa found herself humming along with the phantom melody as she stepped deeper into the maze. The music was magical. Like tiny bells, the notes sparkled in the starlight of the night sky.

How can I know a tune I've never heard? she wondered. A flash of light arched across the sky. She closed her eyes and wished upon it.

Rounding a series of twists and turns, she spotted a single candle flickering upon the stone staircase that spiraled up to nowhere. Rose petals graced each step. *Someone is definitely here,* she thought. Amidst the riot of roses and raspberries that grew entangled together; graced with both thorns and beauty, flowers and aromatic herbs grew all around. The ancient stepping stones spiraled into the very center as Tessa reached the heart of the maze. She saw the altar had been adorned with several tiny candles that cast an ethereal glow. Incense burned slowly, releasing an intoxicating potion of sandalwood that encircled her.

Several items lay there, as if in secret offering. An ornately carved wooden box lay with the lid left open allowed the soft music to spill into the garden. The rich mahogany glimmered in the moonlight. Upon its velvet lining of the deepest blue, rested a most enchanting necklace. Its iridescent stone, resembling an opal or pearl, was held in the iron grip of a gryphon's claw. The silver chain was of the finest quality. Scrolled in perfect script, with sweeping lines of a strong hand, the words to the haunting melody were also laid there for her to find. A single purple rose lay next to the box, with a ribbon tied around its stem. Not a ribbon, but a single narrow strand of soft leather. A hair tie. *Her* hair tie.

"That can't be," she mumbled to herself as she looked around, "I lost that tie while riding the moors with Lachlan more than half a year ago." A chill went down her spine…

A light shone in his eyes as he watched her discover his gifts to her, each one with meaning. His connection to her was never stronger than it was on that night. Had she understood it was he who had been there when the wicked English wind had snatched the leather tie from her hair that day? Had he been there? Aye, he was *always* there. She had never been truly alone on those rides for he had always been nearby. Waiting, watching, guarding what was his. Their whole lives had been that way. He too, spent endless childhood hours in the maze. While Tessa was with her friends of like nobility, he was there tending the roses; watching her all the while. He had taken the tie and kept it for himself; a token from *his Lady* to take with him while in service to the Crown.

Six months had changed him. He'd seen too much death while defending Edward II's borders. He'd watched life slip away while under his hand on more than one occasion. The longer he remained away from Sedgemoor the surer he became that if he made it back alive, he would not live without Tessa. Life was just too short to settle for less.

Though he was from "questionable" heritage, he knew the affection bestowed upon him by the MacLures was genuine. He watched Tessa gather the gifts within the hem of her gown and rush back to the castle in the darkness.

I could go to them, and be honest, he thought, *Though I hold no title, I have enough coin to buy lands. We could build a small keep of our own. We could make it work, if she was willing.*

Birdsong awoke Tessa from her dreams. She so enjoyed those first few moments of wakefulness, when she could lie still and just listen. She relished the feel of her thick down comforter as she curled her toes in a most feline way. The savory aroma of cinnamon scones with fresh strawberry jam brought her from her bed. Tessa stepped to the balcony in her bare feet, the stone was cool to the touch. She cupped the tankard of her favorite concoction with both hands. It was a mixture of crushed filberts, coffee, hot milk and honey. She lightly blew across the potion before she sipped it, deep in ponderous thought. The evening before, washed over her.

"Father would kill me if he knew I'd slipped out yet again," she mumbled as she slurped her brew in a most unladylike fashion. She had felt him there last night, very near though not seen. From under her bed she retrieved the box with all its treasures. She read the words to the song yet again, hanging on every word so boldly written on the golden parchment.

As I walk through this life of mine
I notice the intertwine
Of others

And yes, lately, within the bounds of memory
I look to see if this one still walks
Or is temporary

It's been some time now, and yet she's there
This truefriend, this woman,
My care

I think she walks a different path
That leads to places not seen by me, and still
I know she is there

'Tis good we share this time, we walk we laugh,
To grow another from our pasts,
Together but separate

In you, I live and breathe

As Tessa stepped into her steaming bath drawn for her in front of the blue stone fireplace, she let her thoughts drift. The water caressed her like a lover, in warm and liquid motion. Next to her tub stood a chair draped with a length of toweling and a fresh chemise embroidered with tiny heather and thistle blossoms. Upon the towel lay a roll of parchment sealed with indigo wax. Wiping the soap from her eyes, Tessa reached for it, with a trembling hand.

M'Lady,
I enjoyed watching you come to the garden last eve.
The moonlight cast the most provocative shadows from behind your nightgown...
The years have been good to you, Tessa, very good.
I trust you took pleasure in my gifts to Thee.
I had hoped not to frighten you, but I thought it best to approach you that way,
Alone.
We must talk.
Shall we take a ride over the moors today?
I await your reply, dear Lady.
Your most ardent admirer,
Ruffian

After the midday meal, Ruffian went to the stable to ready the horses. He entered the stalls still choking down his last biscuit.

"Father, I can get the horses ready myself. Go home and get some dinner." Ruffian saw Rod Bardougne place the soft woven blanket on Lachlan's golden back. *He's been exercised,* Ruffian noted as he ran a hand down Lachlan's front leg.

"She's been riding without me."

"Did ya' think her life would stop if ya' left, son?" Rod looked up from the feed trough.

"I didn't expect her to stay locked up in her chamber, no but…."

"Relax. When she rode, she rode alone." Rod handed him the reins, "I better get outta here a'fore I put a wrinkle in those plans of yours." Ruffian noticed his father looking at the blanket he had tucked under his arm.

"She's the Laird's daughter, his only one, son. Don't play, unless you're serious." Rod winked and strolled out into the cool Spring day, whistling as he made his way to their waddle and daub house just east of the stables.

A none too gentle nudge came from behind Ruffian from Thunder who wanted his undivided attention. He readied both horses in record time, leaving

Tessa's sidesaddle sitting right where he'd found it. She hated the thing and to her parent's horror, refused to ride any way but astride. Rod had fashioned her a second saddle; small and hand-tooled with tiny birds and flowers. Though Lachlan was quite a big horse, the saddle seemed to suit both he and Tessa perfectly.

He had received her reply at breakfast, in the castle's kitchens. He ate there, except for special occasions. Jolie was often gone to the weaving house before dawn, so the Bardougne's ate with the castle "help". Though the MacLures saw to Ruffian's education and training, they kept him at a polite distance. He assumed it was because his parents had been of the working class, so he never took it personally. Tormond had a son, Sir Leland, who was their first born. Lee was married and oversaw the properties at Ravensclaw, near Sodbury. He was the heir to the lands and title. Ruffian was content, having been blessed with two families. Jolie and Rod had taught him about nearly all aspects of castle life. He was trained in masonry, design and engineering, land management and botany. He could break a horse and propagate roses, and no one bested him on the practice fields with either lance or sword, though Ethan was quickly gaining ground. He could speak Latin, Italian and French, and play the mandolin. *The only thing I seem to lack is a title attached to my name,* he smirked.

Tessa startled him out of his thoughts as she stumbled into the stables. *So much for grace,* she frowned. Thunder regarded Ruffian with a snort. Lachlan was happily munching away on his oats, when she finally stepped into the hazy, dust-filled stall. Her cheeks were scarlet from the wind outside; her hair already coming down from her braid. She was a mess, and she took his breath away.
    "A wondrous fair day for a ride, is it not?" he bowed regally before her.
    "I got your note."
    "So I see." He led her to Lachlan and took her hand.
    "I don't need your help."
    "Yes you do."

She rolled her eyes and sighed. He knew she'd been riding since she could walk. He never offered to help her before. He grinned the most wicked grin he could muster.

"It's cold out there today. We could just stay here instead, if you like." She noticed the blanket laying in the corner, and a bottle of mead nearby.

"I thought you invited me to ride with you?" He could smell the heather in her hair as she brushed past him. The gentle folds of her cloak did nothing to conceal the woman she'd become. *I have been away too long,* he thought.

It was hard for her to hold his gaze. He looked like a hungry wolf. He seemed to look through her to the private thoughts she'd hidden. She looked away to find herself again. *He's way too close to me. I can't handle this.* She backed up several paces. She could hear him breathing. His scent was an intoxicating mix of man, leather and smoke from the fires outside. She felt herself so wanting to stay; to find out what would happen if she did.

"Are you frightened of me, Tessa?" He stepped closer and touched her, "You are trembling."

"Nay, I'm cold, 'tis all." It was a lie and they both knew it, but Ruffian knew better than to push.

They set out for the moors together. As was their custom, they rode side by side to Grinstead Hill, then all bets were off. They'd race each other to the moors of Dundrennan. It was tradition. Ruffian, being nearly two years older, always won those early contests. *I remember the first time I bested him,* she smiled as she pulled into the lead, *I was eight and he was almost ten.* Ruffian never forgot either…it was the day he fell in love with her.

❀

CHAPTER 3

THE OAK OF DUNDRENNAN

"Tessa, we must speak," Ruffian began as he reined in Thunder underneath the oaks on Dundrennan Moor. She seemed to miss the urgency in his voice. *It's so beautiful. I love coming here in the snow to gather mistletoe for the Yule celebration.* It was a sacred place to the Ancients. One tree, on a gentle hill, stood out among the rest. They had learned the legend of the Enchanted Oak at Elspeth's knee. They were even quizzed on the details; for the lore of the realm was handed down orally so that no one would forget. Each generation took their turn as caretakers of the legends very seriously.

The tree had simply *always* been there. Even the oldest crones in the realm could not remember a time when it hadn't looked *exactly* as it did then; massive, majestic and magical. Those of the Old Religion had worshipped at its base. Pagan sacrifices had been made; allegiances sworn beneath the full of the moon. But that had been life times ago. They worshipped the true Lord now; God of all realms. Still the tree remained, with its secrets locked deep within.

Elspeth had told of a great battle that took place in the valley below. The cries of brave men once filled the land. Defending their homes, masses died. Their blood seeped into the fertile ground, anointing it with life's essence. Through impossible odds, they prevailed and held the land of Dundrennan. From that time on, the site had been a sacred place of courage and miracles. Sunday services were often held there. Babies were routinely brought before the tree for christenings. Weddings were sometimes performed under the can-opy of deep green leaves. Occasionally, a kiss, or something a bit more was sto-len there on gentle summer days. *Here* was where he was going to bear his soul…finally.

Propriety be damned. Baron or Knight, rich or poor; I love her and I'm going to make sure she knows it. Whether she embraces me, or politely dismisses me from her life, I have to know once and for all, he decided.

"Tessa, I would have a word with you regarding your future," he began, "I know it's concerned you that you are nigh twenty and one and as yet, you have not taken a husband." She shrugged and silently scanned the moors.

"Don't worry yourself on my behalf, true friend. I find it understandable that the men in this land find me most curious and a bit bizarre at times. I've heard the whispers behind my back. My gift of intuition scares them, I think. They don't want to be found consorting with a witch of the Old Religion. For crying out loud, those pagan ways died out nearly 500 years ago! The MacLures built upon one of the oldest Christian sites in Dundrennan, do they think it was done without just cause?" She looked away again, to regain con-trol. "I'm sorry. My family is very important to me. I will not have outsiders conjure lies about them, or me. I know people fear what they do not under-stand." Her second sight seemed only to be linked to those in her immediate family, and the Bardougnes, which included Ruffian.

"That is not true. Well, not for the most part." He stepped in front of her to capture her attention. "I know you think no one has asked for your hand, but you are gravely mistaken. Many have come seeking to wed you. Your father has turned each one away. He will not let you go easily. You are most cherished at Sedgemoor," he whispered into her hair.

"Tessa, I have something to tell…."

"Oh! I forgot to tell you!" she interrupted. He dragged his hand through his hair and closed his eyes, *She's killing me, here!*

"Guess what, I mean *who* is coming to visit from a season at court? 'Tis the Baron and Baroness of Stolford and their horrid children, Hester, Belinda and Youghal. Consider yourself lucky, dear one, to have your freedom!" she made a face that would curdle fresh milk.

"My freedom is exactly what I don't want!" he grumbled under his breath.

The moment had passed, as had all the moments before. *I can't tell her now. Obviously the Baron is coming to form an alliance betwixt the Houses of Stolford and MacLure. God, how I'd hate to see Tessa saddled with Youghal Stolford, that goatish, dog-hearted slug. The thought of him touching her, demanding his due; and her submitting to it out of duty to her family is more than I can take. Something will have to be done...*

CHAPTER 4

❀

THE VISIT FROM HELL

Juin 1309
Sedgemoor

Everyone prepared themselves for the arrival of the family de Stolford. Tessa saw her mother down an entire glass of wine before joining the family outside.

"Oh come on now, Elspeth, Westley Stolford is a nice enough fellow!" Tormond swatted her on the behind when she sighed in a long-suffering manner. "We were just never particularly close, since our interests lie in different directions. I was interested in knightly pursuits and Stolford had a weakness for gaming and entirely too much wine." Elspeth hiccuped.

As a young man, the Baron had only moderate family wealth to squander; therefore his *hobby* required he marry quite well. He found his security in one, Roxanne Pinkerton. A spinster at age 35 when they'd met, she was the only child of the very wealthy Pinkertons of Devonshire. It was a match made somewhere *other* than heaven.

The Stolfords arrived with the expected pageantry. Four carriages in all, the Baron and Baroness rode in the first, Youghal, Hester and Belinda in the second, personal domestic staff in the third and luggage filled the fourth. Ruffian expected to hear trumpets sound and doves to be released just to herald their arrival! "Obviously, their time at court has only served to reinforce their sense of self-importance," he muttered.

Tormond had made it a point to ask Ruffian to be present with the family. Tessa was there, in her most sedate attire. *A mousy-brown woolen dress laced up to my chin would surely discourage Youghal's attentions,* she thought. *Where did she dig up that wretched looking thing anyway?* Ruffian thought he'd seen her at her worst...*I guess not.* Tessa's long auburn locks were pulled back and hidden beneath a scarf that Jolie had woven for her last birthday. He had to smile at her attempt to hide her obvious charms. *I hate this.* A nerve began to twitch in his jaw. *Youghal's wealth and position, or future position as soon as the old man was dead means nothing to Tessa, but what of Tormond? He's a good man who loves his daughter. So much, in fact, that he might look past all the distasteful qualities of the Stolfords just to secure her future.*

"MacLure, you old dog! I see Elspeth has been treatin' you well enough!" the Baron called as he and his wife stepped from their carriage. His too-familiar manner always annoyed Elspeth. Tormond let it pass.

"Welcome Stolford, safe trip I take it?" Tormond lightly kissed Roxanne's gloved hand.

"Uneventful, I must say, but pleasant enough I suppose." Westley made a beeline for Elspeth. She begrudgingly held out her hand to receive his slobbery greeting.

"Look what you've done, you idiot! You spattered mud on my gown when you slipped trying to help me from my carriage! You, oaf! Mama!" Hester Stolford yowled. Belinda quietly made her way from the carriage unassisted and followed her bellowing sister into the keep. *Lovely,* Ruffian thought. Last but not least, Youghal roguishly jumped down from the carriage like a hero from a bad play. Walking past everyone, he cut a path straight for Tessa.

"Like father, like son..." Elspeth whispered to Tormond.

Youghal casually tossed his personal satchel to Ruffian. "Haul this up to my chamber right away, there's a good lad," he said without giving Ruffian even a passing glance. When Ruffian just as casually let the bag fall to the ground with a thud, all eyes, including Youghal's turned to him.

"Surely you meant to hand this to one of the domestics," he said innocently enough.

"Am I mistaken, or isn't that what you are, Rascal or Rasputan or whatever your name is?" Youghal shot back.

"*Ruffian* is here at my personal invitation, Stolford," Tormond stepped in, "He is a guest, as you are."

That comment hurt. *A guest? I know I'm not exactly family but that seemed rather cold, didn't it?"* he thought. *If that's how the MacLures feel, it's fine by me. I can be as close or distant as they wish. One thing is for sure; Tessa will not be out of my sight while that slug is roaming the grounds at Sedgemoor!*

As it turned out, Ruffian had his hands full fending off Hester. She eyed him from the doorway like that night's entree'. Her too-full figure seemed to be crammed into the straining seams of her gown. Apparently Hester never missed a meal. It appeared that, by the looks of things, she might have even snitched morsels off Belinda's plate when she wasn't looking! What was even more obvious that she had taken a fancy to Ruffian's shoulder length hair and blue eyes. *So, I'm her version of slumming?* he questioned, *It's going to be a most interesting visit.*

The birds stopped singing and small animals hid, for the Stolfords had come to Sedgemoor.

Dinner was ridiculous. Tessa fended off Youghal as best she could between courses. The man couldn't imagine why she wasn't interested. Not that that fact slowed him down any. Hester kept amused by fondling Ruffian's leg with her own, under the table. He watched as she slowly and seductively tasted each sweet on her desert plate. She rolled the concoctions around her tongue and smacked her full lips. The Baron sipped the mead from his goblet and made small talk. He looked about the great hall nervously. It was obvious that he had something on his mind. Tormond politely excused them both as they retired to his study. The negotiations had begun, and Tessa's world lay in the balance.

I'd like to wipe the smirk off that toad's face! Ruffian reached for another glass of wine.

"Don't you think you've had enough? Tessa murmured.

"Yes, old boy?" Youghal chimed in.

He draped his arm around Tessa's chair and lightly touched the tendril of hair at the nape of her neck. Pushed almost to the limit, Ruffian wasn't sure what made him do it. He had been graciously invited to join them all for dinner. Treated again as a *guest*; probably at the request of Youghal, who so dearly wanted to put him in his place in front of the entire assembly. *I can't stand this. Our fate is being sealed in the other room, and I sit here like an idiot, powerless to change it.* Maybe it was Stolford's taunting sneers. Maybe he was angry with Tessa for putting him in that position, after all, he didn't *want* to be in love with her. Whatever the reason, as the wine finally caught up with him, he decided to take Hester Stolford up on her dirty little game. *I'm never going to be with Tessa now, so what the hell?* He completely missed the satisfied smile on Roxanne Stolford's face.

A part of him wanted to punish Tessa, for turning him into a mad man. He wanted her to hurt, as he was. *I've lost her, I know. In fact, I never really had her at all. As grotesque as Youghal is, he can offer her more than I ever could.* It would be easier that way. He'd betray her openly, and she'd run to the slug. *She'll enter this marriage with Stolford and never look back.* Ruffian could disappear from Sedgemoor. There would be nothing left for him after Tessa had gone. He had enough gold to make his own way. He didn't need the MacLure's charity. *I don't need Tessa.*

"I praythee, m'lady Hester, would you care to accompany me on a moonlit stroll about the castle grounds? The gardens, I hear tell are wondrous fair this time of year," he asked as he stood and offered his arm and a wicked grin. Hester looked to her mother for 'further instructions'.

"By all means, you two young people go on and have a good time on your stroll," the Baroness fairly purred with delight.

Their eyes briefly met as he escorted a giggling Hester from the hall. The hurt he saw there almost crushed him. He had to look away so Tessa wouldn't see the truth reflecting back at her in the candlelight. She sat there a moment, making sure they were well away from the hall before excusing herself from the table. She wouldn't give Ruffian or the Stolfords the satisfaction of running hysterically to her chamber. She was practically numb. The pain was so deep, it had simply seared her senses.

She lay in the darkness, wondering why the world worked as it did.

"Why can't people just marry for love?" she called out to no one, "What has my all-important social standing gained me thus far?" The answers would not come tonight. She clutched her chest and cried out in a muffled sob, thinking she could feel her own heart breaking. In reality she was being made privy to Ruffian's world shattering around him.

He kissed Hester, long and deep under the moonlit sky. *Still too much light, he thought, I can still see her beefy face.* He tried his best to play his part well. He kissed her again, roughly, making her squeal in delight. He knew that at least one of the servants would have to see or hear them. Hester grabbed his tunic, trying to disrobe him right there. The exertion was obviously too much for her stressed bodice, for he heard a seam rip. *Tessa will surely hear of this by morning. Of course, I can't let it go too far. I'm not going to be blamed for ruining the "fair Hester"! By the way she's acting, I think that happened a long time ago and I'm not getting saddled with that banshee for the rest of my life.* He would simply show the girl a good time, then ride away once he knew the charade was complete.

It all seemed like such a logical plan…

CHAPTER 5

❀

A TWISTED TURN OF EVENTS

"The Castle is abed," Jolie said as she sat looking out from her cottage window at the grandeur of Sedgemoor. She couldn't see the candlelight still flickering from Tormond's chamber. Rod marveled at her talent for embroidering without watching what she was doing.

"Blast! Who sharpened these bloody needles?" she slurred, with her index finger in her mouth. Tiny droplets of blood now adorned her work. Rod sat at their worn oak table, repairing a leather bridle for Thunder. He knew that look on her face. Something was going on, and Jolie would not sleep that night, therefore, *would he?*

The shutters and doors stood open, allowing the cool evening breeze to dispel the heat of the day. It also allowed for full view of both the keep and the nearby gardens. Jolie saw her son walking with someone other than Tessa in the moonlight.

"Probably that awful Stolford girl," Rod heard her grumble under her breath.

He noticed she began to rock a bit faster as she sewed on. He grinned and shook his head ever so slightly. When he heard her say something about the tides and moon phases making people do insane things, he decided to leave her to herself. Rod knew better than to try to figure out his wife. She was like a wild and beautiful creature of nature. He knew he'd never tame her, not that he really wanted to. He was just grateful to have had the chance to love her. He often wondered what such a complicated woman ever saw in such a simple man as he.

"Kiss me, wench, I'm tired and I'm going to bed," Rod announced like the lord of the manor. He stood and stretched, before making an ungodly face at the pain in his back. Older than his wife, Rod's years of heavy labor played havoc with his joints and muscles. She laid aside her needlework and reached for him. She placed her hands on the specific points on his shoulders and began gentle pressure until the knots eased and softened.

"I don't deserve you," he moaned in delight.

"I know."

"How can you think of sleeping?" she asked. The massage was over, and now Jolie stood staring at him. Her hands were on her slender hips and she was tapping the toe of her black leather slippers that he had made for her. The keys that hung from her waist on a golden chain jingled. She tried her best to look disapprovingly at him.

"Ignorance is bliss, or so I am told," he grinned.

"No, ignorance is stupidity." *Obviously he has no clue what's at stake here!* She looked upon him with pity; the poor, hapless creature he'd become. She mumbled something about Ruffian as she grabbed her cloak and made her way to the door. Rod reached out a tanned muscular arm toward her, "Jolie."

"He's going to ruin everything!" she snapped.

"It's his life, love, you can't live it for him."

"But Tessa is…"

"Tessa is a very intelligent and strong woman."

"Rod, you don't understand. They *must* join together. It has been predestined."

"If it's predestined then you have naught to worry about. They have no say in the matter."

"That's where you're wrong, husband, free will shall always have its say."

"Hmmm…I guess you're right, what with the whole Garden of Eden fiasco and everything." He smiled again, trying to engage her, but she would not be consoled.

"A time is coming, Rod. Our generation may not see it. God forgive me, but I hope we do not. As surely as I'm standing here, I know it's true. Ruffian and Tessa must wed. The union must take place! There is a threat on the horizon. Those at Sedgemoor will someday need them in defense of some sort of terrible battle."

"So, you're a prophetess now?" Rod knew Jolie had the same sensitivity to people and events that Tessa displayed. There had even been talk of Elspeth, the Lady of the keep, knowing things that were beyond her own grasp, though it was only spoken of in hushed whispers on the back staircases of Sedgemoor. But all this doomsday talk from Jolie was making him a bit edgy.

"Goodnight, husband." Jolie kissed him once again and walked to the weaving house where all was dark and still. He saw sadness in her eyes as she said goodnight. It was a facet of their marriage they had never been able to share. Rod dealt in the here and now of life. With the exception of God, he trusted nothing he could not see, touch or taste for himself. He knew his last comment had crossed the line. He knew, in all the world, *he* should be the one who had faith in her. *She's always right about these things*, he thought, *when will I ever learn to just shut up?* He knew as well as she did; it was an age-old question.

She stepped into the weaving house and lit the beeswax tapers that sat in black iron sconces forged by her husband. *He has never understood my legacy* she thought to herself as she sat down before the tapestry that she'd been working on for weeks. She knew it wasn't his fault. *'Tis true, I am not like others. I should be grateful to be accepted as well as I have been all these years.* Old superstitions ran deep in the land surrounding Sedgemoor.

The familiar rhythm of the loom and shuttle lulled her into a state of blessed relaxation. The tapestry was to be a gift. Jolie worked on it only in her free time. During the day, she was the consummate professional; an artisan pledged to serve the MacLures. But late in the night, she would often slip away from the house and come to the loom. It was a very spiritual thing to weave a masterpiece from nothing but pieces of string and silk. It was also very humbling, because she knew she was not the creator, indeed only a tool. Dark threads and light blended together in a most intimate dance to bring forth the life within the art. Jolie surrendered the fear and the need to control events as she lost herself in the work of the tapestry. She was content to be living in that

place and time, for she knew that too had been pre-ordained. In every generation; there had to be watchers; caretakers of the truths of Dundrennan.

"Burning the midnight oil, mother?" Ruffian stood leaning against the
doorway in a most casual way.

"Straighten your tunic, Ruffian," was all Jolie said as she concentrated on
the weaving.

"I'm leaving at dawn, mother." Ruffian stood up straighter and his tone was
all too serious.

"Business for the MacLures?" she was hoping for a miracle.

"Nay, I'm thinking of building a keep of my own near the north end of the
realm. Justin McKinnon lives near there and he bid me to come visit if I was
ever in the area. He has a fine herd of sheep, I hear."

"You hate sheep, Ruffian."

"I need some time away to think."

"About what?" The loom was now silent. "About how you've come back
only to find the world *hasn't* stopped spinning since you've been gone? About
how Tessa has grown up over the last six months without you here? About you
male ego, or pride or your fear?" Jolie asked.

"I don't need this, mother. You know Stolford is coming to terms with
MacLure tonight. I'll be doing everyone involved a kindness by bowing out
gracefully."

"There is nothing I can say to change your mind?" She seemed to accept
defeat as she stepped to the doorway. *Testing me already, Lord? Before the ink
was even dry on my prayers?* she thought. Ruffian scooped the tiny woman in
his arms and lifted her from the floor in a tremendous hug.

"Sometimes it's best to just walk away, mother. I mean, it was crazy to think
I ever stood a chance anyway! Lairds don't just *give* their daughters and dow-
ries away on a lark. It was a waste of time for me to think of reaching beyond
my lot in life. There's no shame in being of the working class. Serfs and Noble-
men alike respect father for his skills with horses and ironworks. If I can be half
as forthright as he is, I'll be satisfied."

"Very convincing," Jolie smiled, "have you managed to make yourself
believe that pile of dung as of yet?"

"Mother…."

"Cease! This conversation is over, son. I'm tired. Do what you feel is right. I
am well past giving my permission for you to act upon. I believe I lost that

power over you somewhere around the age of ten?" Jolie hugged her son once again. *Amazing! This wasn't the awful scene I had imagined it would be,* he smiled. Ignorance really *is* bliss. *And love will bring him home.* Yet one more mother's prayer ascended heavenward.

CHAPTER 6

❀

DESTINY'S CALL

A soft knock brought Tormond from his thoughts.

"Come."

"May I have a word, Sire?"

"Why so formal, Jolie? We are alone here," Tormond chuckled.

"He's leaving at dawn."

"Stolford? I wish we'd be so lucky."

"Not the Stolfords, Ruffian is leaving Sedgemoor."

"Where can he be off to now? He's only been home a fortnight."

Jolie sat down on one of the twin settees in front of the hearth. Her back was ram-rod straight. Tormond likened her to an animal on alert. He knew this was not a social call paid in the wee hours of the morning.

"It's time, Tormond," she whispered.

"I had hoped to wait a bit longer," he confessed to her.

"Nay, we cannot. It seems as if events are moving faster than we thought they would. Ruffian and Tessa need to know the truth, and they need to know it now. I know none of us planned it this way, but the children have found each other, none the less. It's beyond us, Tormond. All we can do is arm them with the truth and pray for the best."

She stood to leave, confident that the Laird of Sedgemoor would agree with her.

"Goodnight, m'lord."

He stopped her,

"Jolie, I will be the one to tell him of this. 'Twas my charade, and I will be the one to end it."

"As you wish." She touched his hand as she left. *So like Elspeth...*he thought as he watched her go.

Tormond had only half finished his brandy when Tessa slipped silently into his chamber. He was studying a yellowed map of his holdings as he swished the amber liquid within the goblet cupped in his hand.

"What think you of Windmere? 'Tis just a day's ride west of the forest. I think it would be better suited for your brother than Ravensclaw. I seek to move he and his bride a little closer to home; for Elspeth, you understand."

"Father I would have a word with you," she began.

"Apparently, I'm popular tonight," he mumbled.

"What?" she wasn't listening. Her attention was on her own prepared speech.

"Never mind, child, what's so important that it cannot wait till the morn?" he fought to stifle a yawn.

She began to sniffle. Tormond looked closer and saw her reddened eyes.

"Sit. Drink this," he commanded, "Slowly now, you're not used to the strength." *If he only knew how many bottles of mead we have shared in the stables over the years.* She closed her eyes at the memories. As the fire crackled on, its light cast flickering shadows across the oak-paneled walls of her father's study. She opened her eyes and sat staring into the flames. He waited patiently as she finally found her voice.

"Father, I am twenty and one."

"Yes, you are as I recall."

"And I have no husband."

"Not unless I seemed to have missed the wedding," he grinned. Silence once again filled the room as she sat staring at the fire.

"Tessa?" he touched her shoulder gently spurring her on to her point.

"I'm too headstrong," she confessed as she drained her glass.

"You know your own mind, an admirable quality."

"Aye in a man, not in a wench."

"Have I *ever* asked you to be anything other than what you are? And you're not a wench, you're a Lady. You are extraordinary, just as your mother is."

"I play with swords while the *ladies* needlepoint," she snorted.

"It could be worse. At least I know you can protect yourself if need be."

"My intuition scares most."

"A gift from God. It will not scare the man you are meant to marry. He will be of like mind and heart, child. But, no one worthy has stepped forward as of yet, 'tis true enough."

"Nay? Not even *Youghal Stolford*?" she faltered. Tormond did not answer.

"I assume there is still a dowry, should a marriage ever take place?" He nodded. Not saying a word, he moved to his chamber window and looked out over the cliffs.

"Have you someone in mind?" he asked casually.

Through her tears, Tessa confessed her deepest longing to her father, though she left out the events of that evening regarding Hester. Their words carried long into the night. Looking back, it would be one of the closest moments ever shared between them.

"I must think on this, Tessa," he whispered into her hair as he held her in a bear's embrace. He set her away from him yet kept his hands upon her slender shoulders.

"Until I make a decision, you are not to spend time alone with him. At dawn I will send my personal runner with a missive from you explaining all this. Mind me in this, daughter," his face looked grave, "There is so much neither of you understand about the situation. You will have to trust me on this."

Though he was grim, Tessa still saw some spark in his troubled eyes. If it could be done, he would make it so.

ॐ

My Dearest One,

My fate has not yet been sealed. I have approached my father and told him my heart. I don't know what will happen, or if you even care at this point. I love you, Ruffian, God help me. I shall probably be a fool for telling you, but I cannot lie any longer. I have waited for you. You have teased and complimented me. You have stolen kisses since we were children. Could you not see it in my eyes? You are the world to me, but still you do not speak.

Have I been naught but a recreation for you? I thought I could feel a connection between us. Was I so wrong? I watched you leave with Hester. Like a knife it cut me to the core. Your punishment was accomplished most effectively, m'lord. Yet, to my father, I pledged my love for you. If we cannot be, then I choose to be alone.

Circumstances are not what they appear. My father has commanded I not see you again until he deems it prudent. There is some sort of unrest, but I cannot quite name it. He asked us to trust him and be patient. If anyone can help us be together, it is he.

If there was ever a time to declare yourself, my love, now is it. You are under no obligation to me. But I must know the truth of your feelings. I believe I deserve at least that much. Until I hear from you, you shall be ever in my thoughts.

Hold fast,

Tessa

Tormond MacLure slipped into the south tower of his keep. The heavy door squeaked in rebellion as he pushed against it with a battle-weary shoulder. He entered the now desolate chamber at the tower's peak. Dark and musty, the stale air assaulted his nostrils with the lingering essence of heartbreak and death. *Can I really bring myself to relive all this?* he wondered. The tower had been locked and all but abandoned since the incident on All Hallow's Eve.

He lit the candles, still in their holders after all those years. Still half-burnt as they were when he himself snuffed them out so long ago. Their glow warmed him a bit. He sighed in the stillness that surrounded him. Life had indeed gone on. *There has been joy and laughter and life…But now, what transpired so long ago must be faced and dealt with. The children are children no longer. I always knew the truth would need be told one day.*

The bed still sat in the old chamber. The sheeting had been stripped and burned of course. Only a rotting straw tick laid there now. Tormond shook his head slightly, as if to dispel the echoes of the past. He could still hear her screams. She prayed, she *begged* for mercy. She lain right there and begged him to save her child. A single tear escaped his eyes. He quickly dashed it away. *So, so long ago….*

Wanting to be gone from that place as soon as he could, Tormond set about his task. He stepped quickly to the hearth, cold and lifeless as the rest of the room, and reached inside the firebox. Feeling about, he finally laid hold of the loosened stone within. Moving it aside, he brought forth the box that held the answers to so much. He slipped back into his own bedchamber just before dawn. Elspeth had been asleep for hours, unaware of this latest turn of events. The waning moon bathed her face in an ethereal light. *"God, how I love this woman,* he thought, *if Ruffian feels the same about Tessa, then I have to do this.*

Hoping to get at least an hour or two of sleep before the morn, he tried his best to move quietly about their chamber. He had just undressed and slipped into bed, when she jabbed him in the ribs. Elspeth's face was but a hair's breadth from his.

"Are you going to tell me what had you roaming the castle all night long?"

"In the morning, love," he murmured as he began to nuzzle her neck.

"I had a dream about Tessa."

"Was she married to *Youghal?*"

"Actually, no. We were dancing at some sort of feast, and I heard her scream."

"Tessa is fine, just a dream." He stroked her hair.

"They are never *just dreams*, darling. I tossed and turned all night, bits and pieces of scenes danced in my head. Some were memories, but others…" he silenced her with his warm kiss.

"In the morning, Elspeth. Can we not have these last few hours together before everything changes?" His cryptic question only served to further her unrest, but she knew her husband well.

"It is Ruffian," she stated rather than asked, "Does he know yet?"

"Nay, I just retrieved the box from the tower." He sighed as he fiddled with the ribbons on the front of her chemise. "I tell you, the heaviness and oppression in that room hit me like a stone wall when I entered it. Maybe ending this falsehood will bring peace to all of us, both the living and the dead." Tormond then proceeded to thoroughly make love to his Lady. Knowing the pain of loss only too well, they rejoiced in the blessing that they had been allowed to survive and endure together.

The runner had been dispatched at dawn with the missive from Tessa. He headed straight for the loft over the stables where both Ruffian and Ethan slept. But before he got there, one of Sedgemoor's guests offered to deliver the message instead.

"I cannot believe the Laird has you up at dawn to run his errands while he sleeps warm in his bed," Youghal Stolford clucked with feigned pity, "Why don't you let me deliver the message? Is it for Sir Ethan or that Ruffian chap?"

"'Tis for Sir Ruffian, m'lord," the boy shivered.

"Excellent! Why, I was just meeting him here to go for a morning ride. I will be sure to give it to him, and you, poor boy, can climb back in your bed," Youghal smiled.

"Thank you, m'lord!" and the boy quickly scampered back to the keep.

"No trouble at all, I assure you."

CHAPTER 7

SPIRALS

"Are you insane?" Ethan wiped the crust from his eyes as he sat up in bed.

"What? No, Are you insane, *M'lord?*" Ruffian snorted as he packed his things in a dark leather satchel.

"We are not on the battlefield now, brother."

"Aye, I wish we were. War is simple. You see the adversary. You kill him and move on."

"Is that really what you want life to be like? Or, is this about someone in particular?"

"Blast the Stolfords to Hell, I say," Ruffian mumbled.

"That Belinda is sort of…cute," Ethan mused.

"Do not even *think* about getting involved with that hideous family or I swear I'll come back and beat you senseless." At that, Ethan laughed and fell back into bed.

"Hmm…from what I hear, that Hester was…"

"Shut up," Ruffian snapped.

"You'll not get far, I wager."

"Watch me."

"You know damn well this place has a hold on us. We are part of this land, or it is part of us, I'm not sure which," Ethan shrugged.

"There's nothing to hold me here now."

"What will you bet me?"

"You'd lose, little brother."

"So, where exactly are you going, just in case I should get fed up with my life and wish to run away from home too?" Ethan grinned.

"I am not running."

"Okay, just where are you *not* running to?"

"McKinnon's keep, to the north," he finished stuffing the bag, laying his journal carefully on top, "I already told mother in case they need to contact me."

"Ooh! I would've loved to have been a fly on the wall during *that* conversation!"

"Mother understood, and told me to do what I needed to do."

"You *are* kidding, right?" Ethan's eyes sparkled in merriment, "Have you forgotten how she handled us as children? She'd let us *think* we had gotten our own way, only to sit scratching our heads later as to how we ended up doing exactly as she wished in the first place!"

"Women are devious creatures," Ruffian admitted.

"Aye, and our mother wrote the book!" Ethan laughed.

"I shall miss you." Ruffian was suddenly serious.

"You're not going to hug me, are you?" Ethan's face went solemn.

"Go back to sleep, maggot."

"Ah, there's the brother I know and love." He rolled over and snuggled deeper into his blanket.

"I love you too," Ruffian whispered as he reached the bottom of the ladder.

The morning brought Tessa from her chamber. She had finally slept, but there had been no true rest. At dawn, Tormond's runner had taken her letter. *Why haven't I heard from him?* She paced like a caged cat across the cold, stone floor of the upper landing. An hour passed, then another. The servants began to mill about the great hall. Tessa noticed them whispering. A girl with stringy, black hair looked up at her and giggled. She could hear snippets of conversation over the noise of tables and benches being moved for the meal; *Someone being groped in the garden, a ripped bodice, two people rolling around near the reflecting pools.*

"How could he do this?" she whispered.

Tessa ran to the stables. Her cloak did nothing to warm the chill that ran through her. She noticed Thunder was not in his stall. Her eyes were beginning to blur as she saddled Lachlan. *I have to get out of here!* She climbed atop the nervous animal and raced toward the moors. She left her tangled thoughts behind as she followed the well-worn paths she had once ridden with Ruffian. There was no where to go that didn't remind her of him. Jolie watched Tessa ride away from Sedgemoor.

"I hope it's not too late," she murmured.

Tessa reined Lachlan in as they reached the ancient oak. She slipped from the saddle and scrambled up the hill to the tree. She touched the gnarled bark and closed her eyes. When she found the spiral carved deeply into the wood, she smiled through the pain. She traced the never-ending lines with trembling fingers.

"It means our kinship will never end," she remembered Ruffian telling her after he'd carved it there.

"You promised you'd never leave."

High in the tree, where the branches began to fan out from the trunk, was a hidden knothole. They had hidden their treasures there as children. Secret messages had been passed via the tree for years. No one knew of the hiding place, but Tessa and Ruffian. She rounded the tree and reached up awkwardly to feel inside. *Mayhap you put your letter here?* Her head told her it would not be there. Her heart told her that miracles still happen.

Ruffian shook his head as he watched her from high above, on the cliffs of Dundrennan. It had been his only mistake. *I should've ridden out just after parting ways with that cow, Hester!* He knew the servants had seen plenty. His plan had worked beautifully. *Tessa surely hates me now, so what ever possessed me to leave it for her?* It was for the same reason Tessa was there at the tree. The ties just went too deep. He thought she might find it months or even years from now, a symbol of what once was alive, now dead and gone. But there she was....

He watched as she pulled the purple rose from the hiding place. He had confessed that the purple roses were his favorite, and that he had raised that particular variety just for her. A thorn pierced her hand and a crimson ribbon of blood trickled onto her sleeve. He saw her cry out and crumple to the ground before him. He sighed deeply and turned Thunder to leave.

"Going somewhere?" Tormond asked from the path, "Tell me, boy, do you *enjoy* hurting her so?" His voice was eerily calm, but Ruffian understood the warning in his grey eyes.

"Laird MacLure, Sir, trust me when I say I never meant things to turn out this way. I *had* to hurt her. She'd not marry another unless she *hated* me. I thought to make things easier for you! This way, I shall be the villain, not you. I know you must wed her to Stolford. I want you to know I fully understand, Sire."

"You understand nothing, you presumptuous clod! You are both so quick to play the martyr in all this, aren't you? Neither of you even have a clue as to my decision regarding young Youghal. Think you both I am daft?" Tormond's horse stamped nervously at the ground, reacting to his master's mood. "Do you know that Tessa came to me herself last night to plead your case? And this, *after* you left to dally with Hester! She respectfully told me she would never marry Stolford or anyone else for that matter. She would rather face the stigma of spinsterhood rather than marry falsely. Why? Because for some insane reason, she's in love with you!" Tormond boomed, "And you, my boy, disappoint me. Were you honestly going to ride out of here, never to be seen again? Did you forget your family is here, and what of us? Don't we deserve better? Would you really give her up so easily? What a *grand* gesture, to give up your own happiness for Tessa's greater good," he scoffed.

"I'm sorry, Sir," Ruffian said quietly.

"Youghal? Surely you jest, sir!" Tormond hooted, "Also, I must say I find it rather bad form to reject Tessa's missive to thee. You had only to wait for me to arrange a way to join you two."

"Reject what missive? I've not heard from Tessa at all, but I would hazard to guess 'twould not be words of endearment after my actions last night."

"And what was that pitiful display of 'slap and tickle' with Hester in the garden? A purely amateur move, in my opinion," Tormond commented as he looked out over the bluff.

"It worked, didn't it?" Ruffian mumbled.

"It failed, miserably!" Tormond shot back. "Don't you know that a love lost, is the hardest to forget? You've managed to worm your way into her heart forever!" Ruffian smiled slightly.

"Why are you smiling?" Tormond grumbled.

"I don't know."

"Ah! Come along, Knight, I'm afraid it's time to face the music," he commanded as he turned his steed to head for Sedgemoor.

By the time the two had returned to the keep, the Stolfords, and their servants, were packed up and leaving Sedgemoor. They were heading back to court, in defeat.

"I pity that poor Belinda," Tormond sighed, "she's the only decent one in the bunch." Hester was carrying on about her broken love affair with a "lowlander", and Roxanne Stolfords eyes cast daggers at both men as they rode past. Youghal would not meet Ruffian's eyes, but pretended to inspect the condition of his manicure, instead. As they pulled out of sight, Youghal patted the folded letter he had tucked away in his tunic and smiled.

"Await me in my study, Ruffian," Tormond said as he tossed the reins to Rod in the courtyard. His words were cold. *I'm dead*, he thought. He looked to Rod for some reassurance. Rod looked away. *So is this it? Am I to be banished?* Ruffian walked toward the keep as Rod led the horses to the stables. This day would change their lives forever.

Jolie found Tessa in the abbey garden. She was praying in the center of the labyrinth. Jolie walked the stone path silently, searching for the right words to say. *I knew this day would come. Help me to be the person you need me to be, Lord.* She gently touched Tessa, to let her know she was no longer alone.

"He's gone," Tessa wiped her eyes. She was still clutching the rose with her bloodstained hand.

"It appears so," Jolie whispered.

"He never loved me."

"You know that's a lie."

"I don't know what is falsehood and what is truth any longer."

"Mayhap no one knows. You were praying just now, were you not?" Jolie pointed to the altar.

"Aye, 'tis all I have left."

"'Tis all you need, child." Jolie gathered the girl in her arms. They sat and rocked back and forth on the stone bench in the center of the labyrinth until Tessa's sobs lessened. The wind was cool. It swirled, and caused the flowers to dance around them. Both women drew their strength from the sanctuary within the garden.

"Come, your father wishes to see you in his study."

"I've heard all his lectures before."

"Nay, you'll hear no lecture. This day has being pre-ordained, child. Your kinship with Ruffian has led directly to this moment in time. Come. I'll not leave your side," Jolie assured her as they followed the spiraling path back to the abbey gate.

CHAPTER 8

❀

LEGACY

Elspeth watched as Jolie led Tessa into the study. *Doesn't she have her hands full with her own brood? She need not concern herself with mine.* Elspeth's eyes narrowed like a lioness with her cubs. As if Jolie could hear her thoughts, she looked at Elspeth questioningly. *What is her problem? Is it my fault I should know where to find Tessa? Mayhap the Lady should pay more attention to her daughter.*

"M'lady, I have brought Tessa in from the gardens."

"Thank you, Jolie, I will see to her now."

The weaver bobbed slightly in curtsy and moved to the far side of the table to sit with Rod, Ruffian and a confused Ethan. It looked as if the MacLures and Bardougnes were about to face off in some sort of battle. Father Bryan, Sedgemoor's priest was seated at the far end of the table, with his eyes closed. He mouthed secret words no one could here except God himself. *Oh my, this is serious,* Tessa said to herself.

"Why did I have to come?" Ethan was asking his father, "I did nothing wrong here."

"Hush, boy," Rod whispered in the stifling hot room, "This is family business and as part of this family, you will stay and listen."

Tessa seated herself beside her mother. *What is going on? Is Ruffian to be banished for his encounter with Hester 'neath my father's nose?* she wondered. She could not look at him, though she felt his eyes upon her.

"Take off that cloak, dear, your cheeks are flush," Elspeth said. Tessa peeled off the black cloak to reveal a dark green, velvet gown. The colour complimented her hair and eyes beautifully. The needlework on the bodice and sleeves was exquisite. Tiny seed pearls danced upon the fabric, entwined with embroidered vines of English ivy. Jolie smiled as both boys took a belabored breath. If it was one thing Jolie could do, it was create visions from the fabric. The unwanted attention only made Tessa feel worse. *Is it hot in here, or is it just me?* she wondered, *and why are the Bardougnes here? Are we to air all our dirty linens in front of them?* Elspeth patted her daughter's had as they all waited in tense silence.

"You want to tell me what in blazes is going on?" Ethan hissed to Ruffian, "What did you do to her?"
"Shut up, Ethan," Ruffian murmured.

Tormond finally made his way to his study just before the mid-day meal. Under his arm, he cradled a dark wooden box. The box looked old but sturdy, with wrought iron corner brackets and a nasty looking lock adorning the front of it. He looked at the assembly before him and reverently placed the box upon the table.
"Leave us," he commanded the servants. They quickly scurried from the room, shutting the heavy door behind them.

Lost in his own thoughts and memories, Tormond absently caressed the well-worn box in front of him. A subtle clearing of his wife's throat brought him back to the present.
"This day is one I have dreaded. It marks the ending of one life..." Tormond began,
"Oh, God," Ruffian breathed.
"...and the beginning of a new one for us all."
The children looked confused. Jolie's eyes began to mist as Rod reached for her.
"Be strong now, darlin', we aren't losing him just yet." She nodded and blew her nose.

"The things in this box have been hidden away for over twenty years. 'Twas not done to hurt you, Ruffian. I meant to protect both you, and this hold. Though you may not agree after hearing the tale, I did what I thought was best in an impossible situation." Ruffian merely nodded at this, not willing to comment as yet. *I trust him with my life. I know he'd never intentionally harm my family or me.* He had pledged his very life to protect and defend the MacLures the day he was knighted. *Nothing will change my allegiances,* he told himself. Tormond unlocked the box.

He carefully laid the contents upon the table. Ruffian's brow knit together in confusion. Ethan's eyes widened when he spied the jewels. Tessa's attention was caught by the signet ring of tarnished silver. It was embedded with amethysts, her favorite stones, on either side of the gryphon that graced the face of the ring. Beside the ring lay three yellowed and brittle parchments. Two were open, but the other remained sealed with a drop of indigo wax and the gryphon's mark. The last item was a bejeweled dagger, looking as if it was made of gold. There was something inscribed upon the blade in French. They gazed at the treasure before them, then looked to Tormond for explanation. They listened carefully as he began to unravel the shrouded past.

"Ruffian, do you remember coming to live at Sedgemoor?" Tormond asked.

"Nay, m'lord, I do not. Mayhap because I was so young when my parents sent me here," he offered.

"You have no idea *how young*, son. That is the story you were told because I commanded it. Very few knew the truth of your appearance at Sedgemoor. The others that had such knowledge, except for those in this room are all dead. The story was a good one. It was plausible. No one dared question the Laird and his Lady about the *new arrival* at the castle. Of course there were those who concluded you were my bastard son from some secret tryst. It happens oft enough in these times, I suppose. My Elspeth knew the truth of it, so I let the rumors continue. All the more protection for you, lad. When you reached the age when you wanted to return home to your parents, I had to tell you they were dead. Though I knew it hurt you, it was not a lie. In truth, they were gone, and you had been entrusted to us." Tormond hesitated. Jolie sat there silently with tears streaming down her face. He felt for her. She had served them well, above and beyond what they had the right to ask of her. He hated to cause her this pain, but he continued,

"The truth of it, son, is that you were born here. You drew your first breath in the South tower chamber. It was also where your real mother breathed her last. Jolie, Elspeth and I alone witnessed your birth."

Tessa's mouth nearly dropped to the table. *True, Ruffian has always been there, as far as I can recall, but I thought I just couldn't remember that far back.* Both boys sat there, speechless. Ruffian's head was spinning. Everything he thought he was, was a lie. *Of course I always knew the Bardougnes weren't my real parents, but to have been born here?*

"I would hear the whole story now, m'lord," he demanded.

"You will, but first…" placing the ring on Ruffian's hand, Tormond looked into his eyes, *so like his father's,* he thought. "You are Rapheal La Quesnay, heir to the title and holdings at Quesnay castle. Know you this, son, the kingdom you hold, and always have held, are vaster than you can imagine. There is no question of your suitability for our daughter's hand. Though be sure, we judged you not upon your wealth, but on your character."

The ring flashed upon Ruffian's tanned hand. It was heavy silver. It cast purple apparitions around the room. It was a signet ring used to seal documents, but more than that, it signified the *Laird* or Lord of the manor. Ruffian examined the La Quesnay crest upon the ring face. It displayed a powerful gryphon with its wings outstretched. Surrounding the creature were the words, *Soyez deplace par des reves,* "Be moved by dreams". He looked at Tessa. *Can this really be happening?* She smiled gently, as if in answer.

"Adrian La Quesnay was the best friend I ever had," Tormond began as they all got comfortable around the hearth. Like a great bard of old, Tormond revealed the true tale of Ruffian's life.

"I came to know the La Quesnays when I was sent there to foster at age seven. I know it sounds a bit harsh, but sending young boys elsewhere to be trained for knighthood is still practiced to this day, though no longer at Sedgemoor. I was afraid to go live with strangers, but when I got there I met Adrian. We were roughly the same age. He became like a brother to me. He grew to be a wonderful man and even better friend. I loved him very much," Tormond smiled at the memory of the boyhood years they'd spent together.

"After our journey from squire to knight, we earned our spurs together. At age seventeen, we were ordered by the Crown to tend to some nasty business near Normandy. An infidel named Breac and his followers were terrorizing their way through the countryside. They murdered women and children for the mere sport of it. King Edward I wanted it to cease, and he wanted us to stop them. We commanded a contingent of forty men. It was our first real chance to prove ourselves as knights. Of course, we jumped at the chance! We couldn't wait to fight."

"What of my mother?" Ruffian asked. Tormond gently picked up the dagger from the table and brought it to the group. The jewels seemed to mesmerize them all, as he continued the tale.

"We arrived in Normandy with the rain. It was a mess. Of course, Breac had moved on by then, so we were forced to follow in his wake of murder and rape. Our thoughts of glory were washed away by the mud, filth and carnage that ran rampant. There was surely more death in the land than life." Tormond had to take a moment to breathe, *No one should ever know firsthand the horror we had to deal with.*

"We'd been marching for twenty-six days when we finally located the whore-monger and brought him to his knees. His men, mostly foreign mercenaries, scattered to the wind when they saw their leader's head on a pike. We were bringing our men toward the coast in order to cross back over to English soil, when we came upon the village of Beau Monde. The name means *Beautiful World.* But by the time we got there, it was in ruins. The smoke was still drifting from the embers. I remember a dog howling forlornly over the charred body of its master. We saw no sign of life. Breac's mercenaries were heading to their homelands, but often left no stone unturned in their quest for coin and a good night of defilement. It was unlike anything I've seen before or since, thank God."

"Man is truly the most beautiful and most barbaric of all creatures," Jolie murmured. Tormond took a drink from his tankard to bathe his parched throat. The dagger was still in his hand as he continued.

"As we searched the village for survivors, Adrian called to me from a half-standing house near the center of town. I found him there with a girl. She was standing there in a fog, really. I don't think she could sense or feel anything except fear. Her family lay dead around her. Her clothes were torn almost completely from her thin body. She tried to hold the tatters together as best she could, for modesty sake. She was shaking uncontrollably. Surely she thought the raping was not over. From within the rags that had been her clothes, she produced a dagger. She wielded it frantically in front of us. It was covered with blood. Apparently she had gotten a few good licks in, before the men overpowered her. We couldn't believe they hadn't stolen it too, but I suppose the blood covered the jewels embedded in the hilt. When we stepped closer to her, she panicked and nearly slit her own throat rather to endure one more atrocity. Adrian spoke quickly in the French-country dialect she was accustomed to and reassured her we were there to help her. She was like a perfect rose, cruelly crushed by the hand of the enemy. I can honestly say I'd never seen such raw pain in my life. We both became men that day, for all glimpses of boyish innocence were gone."

"What was her name?" Tessa asked, as tears streamed down her cheeks. She had been watching Ruffian's face during the story. It was if they had both been there, the anguish of it was so real.

"Her name was Journey deau Jordaine," Elspeth said, "she was a dear girl."

"Since we were in command, Adrian and I decided to bring her home with us. We spent that day burying her people and collecting what little was left of her belongings. We set out for home that very night. We knew she couldn't stay there one more moment. The men in our company were immensely protective of her. They would've gladly died in her defense, as would I," he squeezed Elspeth's hand.

Ruffian sat there in rapt attention, as Tormond described the mother that he would never know.

"Journey was beautiful, with her soulful eyes and delicate bones; almost like a wee bird. Adrian bathed her and dressed her in his spare tunic and leggings. Their enormous size made her appear childlike, as I recall, but Adrian was totally smitten with her. She seemed to only trust him. He never left her side during our traveling. I admit, I was at first beguiled by her sweetness, but he made it perfectly clear she was going to be his alone." Tormond laughed and kissed Elspeth's hand. "As it turned out, God had other plans for me. There was a young girl awaiting me in Dundrennan." Tessa smiled as she looked at her mother.

"Adrian took Journey home to Quesnay castle. Though society dictated that he should marry only one of noble blood, he made it clear he would marry Journey or naught at all. He got no argument from his parents for they fell in love with her on the spot. I cannot say the same for Adrian's brother, Reginald. As the second son, Reginald knew he'd only inherit a pittance compared to the title that would go to Adrian. Hoping that Adrian would befall misfortune on the battlefield, Reginald was not happy to welcome his brother home. In a fortnight, they were to be married. The Barony of La Quesnay rejoiced over their happiness. His parents were anxious for grandchildren and hoped a boy would be born to secure the future of Quesnay castle. After the nuptials, I returned home to Sedgemoor to begin a life of my own. It was then I married Elspeth."

Elspeth took up the tale from there. Tormond sat down near the hearth and handed the dagger to Ruffian. It was a weighty weapon, but finely crafted.

"It wasn't long, six months or so, before we received word that Journey was with child. The La Quesnays were so relieved, for Adrian's father was in ill health and declining quickly. We sent Artemis there to help with his healing herbs and poultices, hoping it would make a difference. It was a comfort to Adrian's parents that another generation was secure before their passing. However, it was at that point that all hell broke loose between Adrian and Reginald. Journey herself had written me about one particular argument between the two brothers when Reginald had found out about the baby. Reginald accused Adrian of defiling the House of La Quesnay with a commoner's blood. He swore no 'mongrel children' of theirs would ever sit over the House, that it would happen over his dead body. She said that Adrian made it very clear that could be arranged. Reginald, being both bully and coward, decided to back off, but Journey confessed to me that she was very afraid of him."

"As the months passed, I received missives telling me of the troubles surrounding Quesnay castle," Tormond said. "Adrian's father died quite suddenly in his bed, after seeming to recover from his illness. Artemis was perplexed, and returned home quickly, saying there was evil afoot there. Reginald invited half the countryside to the funeral then proceeded to accuse Adrian of murder in front of them. The despicable trash he spewed about Journey in front of all that were present was more than Adrian would stand for. Several cattle on La Quesnay land had died from poisoning. Horses had been stolen. The last straw was when Journey was nearing her time. Adrian's mother befell a 'terrible accident'. She fell down the turret stairs in the middle of the night, snapping her neck. What was bizarre was that the staff swore that Madame La Quesnay would never leave her chamber at night, because she feared darkness. At that, Adrian summoned two of his men and sent them here with Journey. He stayed there at Quesnay to deal with Reginald. We found out later, it took nearly a week for them to reach us. The weather was most foul for October. Her pains had started two days before their arrival. She was so sick by the time they reached us."

Jolie picked up the tale. Ruffian watched his mother begin to pace as she spoke.

"That night, there was a terrible storm brewing in the west. The winds were most fierce and the smell of rain was all around us. As the guards began to close the gates for the night, a call rang out from the battlements, 'Riders approaching!' Three riders, their cloaks billowing wildly behind them, reached the gate just as the rain began to fall. They carried the La Quesnay banner, and so they were allowed to enter."

"I approached them in the bailey," Tormond said, "and was nearly upon them before I spotted Journey, heavy with child, and about to fall from her mount in exhaustion. I caught her just as she collapsed, and carried her into the keep. Elspeth was waiting at the door. Her guard met us in the great hall and told us of the trouble at Quesnay. Adrian had sent her there to keep her safe from Reginald who was in some sort of bewitchment that had addled his mind. They laid a pack on the table from Adrian and told me the contents would explain everything. I instructed Elspeth to take the pack to our chamber and I carried Journey to the South tower after hearing from the guards that a contingent of Reginald's men were less than an hour behind them. I knew they had been sent to eliminate the Lady and the babe once and for all," Tormond hesitated, "I would've died to protect her, Ruffian, you must know that!"

"I was sent for to make ready for the birthing," Jolie began, "I was young, only sixteen, and newly married to Rod. Upon coming to Sedgemoor I had told Lady Elspeth that I had knowledge of midwifery. I met the others in the South tower. Journey was so small and frail I feared the child would not survive. Her screams filled the chamber."

"It tore me apart," Tormond said, "I could do nothing but pray that my men could hold off the attack from Reginald's men, and that God Almighty would spare the dear, wee soul. 'Hold them off as best you can, Cedric,' I called to my Captain as Jolie gave Journey a calming potion to drink and prepared to deliver the wee one who so desperately wanted life. We could hear the battle begin outside. The sickening screams told me some of my men were dying in an attempt to preserve the precious life within the tower. I offered up a quick prayer for their souls as well as for our own. And yet the storm raged on."

"Tormond and I sat near Journey, stroking her sweating brow," Elspeth said. "She knew what was happening even if we refused to believe it ourselves. 'My friends,' she whispered, 'Things are not well with me, I fear. Reginald seeks to kill the babe. You must not let this happen. In my dreams I have seen this child. He has been sent to guard our kingdoms. He must live. I feel the blood escaping, as I grow weaker. Would you promise a dying woman something?" she asked. "I told her she was young and she would get through this. I held her hand as another pain gripped her," Elspeth cried, "Then Journey said 'Promise me you will protect my child. Adrian sent along all the papers needed to prove his title, but this is all I have to give him.' She produced a richly jeweled dagger from her cloak. 'Twas my father's,' she explained between pains, 'Tis the one thing the soldiers did not manage to steal that day in my village. Tell my son that his mother was no *commoner*, she hissed through clenched teeth."

"With a primal moan, unlike anything I'd ever heard, Journey brought forth a son. Jolie held the perfect specimen within her shaking hands. He was beautiful; fully formed with all his fingers and toes. His hair was a downy feathering of honey gold like Journey's. But he breathed not. It would seem that Reginald's plan had succeeded. Journey looked up with bloodshot eyes to her son. We could tell she would not live long. She smiled and touch his still-warm brow and said, 'His name shall be Jordan, after my family, but he shall sit over the House of La Quesnay.' She took the bundle into her trembling arms and softly kissed his head. Elspeth looked to me in bewilderment. Journey did not realize he was gone. I shook my head ever so slightly. I knew in a matter of minutes, mother and son would be together again. We let her revel in the moment, however brief it would be. She took a deep breath and sighed contentedly. A gentle smile played upon her lips, and then she was no more. I hissed at Elspeth, 'That murdering demon has won after all.'"

"But then I called out, you are in haste, m'lord!" Jolie smiled. "My hand was on Journey's abdomen. 'There is yet life in this womb, Sire! Hand me that dagger, quickly now!'

"I obeyed her command, stunned at what she was about to do," Tormond added, "With the precision of an artist, Jolie sliced open Journey's belly. Steam rose from the wound. Jolie's eyes grew wide as she reached inside the cavity. Elspeth cried out and looked away, horrified to see Journey filleted like an animal after the hunt. We could hear the men fighting just outside the chamber door. 'If there's life, wench, then you best be quick about it!' I yelled to Jolie.

Just then, she lifted another babe from Journey's still form. He was perfect, like his brother, but this one was squirming! Jolie wiped the babe off and wrapped him quickly in Journey's cloak. Elspeth took him and darted down the back staircase to our chambers."

"The men burst through the door at that moment," Jolie said, "only to see Journey lying there, covered in blood. She was holding her dead son in her arms."

"I told them, 'Your too late, lads…'Tormond said, 'You'll have no victims to put to your blades today. Now, you can either lose your own lives in the bargain, or you can return to Quesnay and report to Reginald that his damned objectives have been accomplished.' His men decided to leave with their heads still intact. We let them leave. My hope was that Adrian had already killed his lowlife brother in the meantime. Once Reginald was gone, we could return his son to him. He would be devastated about Journey, but we knew he'd be a loving father."

There was silence in the study. They all looked to one another, but the tale was overwhelming.

"I am a twin?" Ruffian was astounded. Tessa moved to his side and wrapped him in her arms. The emptiness of a twenty-three year loss washed over them all.

"I left Jolie and Artemis to prepare the two for a christian burial," Tormond said, "I quickly joined Elspeth in our chambers. She was sitting there, rocking and softly singing to the wee soul asleep in her arms. Leland was four summers old at that time, and Elspeth had been told she'd never bare another child. After seeing Journey die before our eyes in childbirth, that truth was driven home. Oh, how she wanted to keep you! Elspeth hummed a soft melody through her tears. As she rocked, she told me she had given you a name."

"We had no way of knowing how long it would be before we could return you safely to your father," Elspeth began, "And we knew you needed to be christened, to be recognized by the church. So I named you Rapheal La Quesnay. Raphael means *God has healed*. I knew, in time, God *would* heal this horrible injustice.

"A week later, I tried to get a message to Adrian," Tormond said, "I wanted to explain all that has transpired on All Hallows Eve, but my runner returned with the parchments unopened. We found out that Reginald had killed Adrian that very night. Reginald thought, with his family dead, there would be no dispute his right of the Barony. This game was becoming more deadly by the moment. I knew we could not raise you as our own. Reginald was no fool. You would've been a target, as would we all."

"The MacLures asked us to raise you," Rod spoke for the first time since the tale had begun, Jolie was young but old enough to become a mother. As a member of the working class, we tried our best to make you a jack of all trades. As our son, you were free to learn from all the servants. Both the Laird and I knew you would need all this training in order to manage your vast holdings one day." Elspeth looked away, but Tormond saw the pain that the old wounds caused on her face.

"We gave you over to Jolie soon after your birth. It was one of the hardest things we've ever done. Two years later, God blessed us with Tessa, our miracle baby. We all worked together to hide your true identity until you were old enough to face Reginald yourself. He has no idea you even exist. We continued on with the story when you wished to return to your family. We knew it still was not yet safe to reveal the truth," Tormond finished with a sigh.

"Why he is not called Raphael?" Tessa asked. The elders in the room exchanged amused glances and the Tormond explained,

"Why daughter, that was all *your* doing. When Raphael came into the public eye here at Sedgemoor, you were but three summers old. You could not yet pronounce Raphael. Instead it came out some garbled form of *Ruffian*. At first we thought it merely cute, but then we thought to use it as just one more way to bury his identity. Since the word 'ruffian' is rather derogatory in nature, son, it was one more way to distance you from us, by way of social standing. You lived with the servants. We had to keep the truth from reaching Reginald at all costs. I'm afraid the cost was rather dear to you. We are truly sorry if anything we've done ever made you feel 'less-than'. Make no mistake, our love for you is genuine."

CHAPTER 9

❀

GUARDED BOXES

The box still lay open, its contents splayed across the table in the study.

"These are the things that were sent with Journey the night you were born," Tormond explained, "I guess Adrian knew there was at least a chance that his own life was in danger. His hope was that these things would be enough to secure your position as his heir. The dagger, as you know, was your mother's. The Jourdaine name and motto is inscribed on the blade," he added. The blade had been wiped clean right after Ruffian's birth, but a tiny droplet of Journey's blood still lingered. It had dried upon a jewel in the dagger's hilt. Ruffian grasped the dagger tighter and closed his eyes. The depth of such sacrifice astounded him.

"Of course, the ring you now wear was your father's. The gryphon appears upon his banner as well. I have kept it among my belongings and will surrender it to you today. As for the parchment there, you can see it was sealed with that ring by your father's own hand. I must confess, there was many times we were tempted to read it to see if there be anything there to help us proceed with your care. The other parchments are both your parent's marriage writ, signed by the Bishop of Sodbury, and your christening record witnessed by our own priest here at Sedgemoor. If you recall, last year Elspeth gifted you with a necklace before you went to fight for Edward II. It was a stone in the grip of a gryphon's claw. That too, had been in this box. It had been a gift from Adrian to

Journey on their wedding day." Ruffian looked to Tessa as she pulled the pendant from under the neckline of her gown.

"I wish to see the place they are buried," Ruffian said as he raked his hand through his hair. The afternoon had been exhausting. *Too much to fathom,* he thought, *A life I knew nothing of surrounded me all this time. I don't know whether to grieve or be angry for the lies. God help me, but I'm relieved, even happy because I can make Tessa mine with no hesitation. I guess I have the rest of my life to figure out who I really am.*

"As you know, the Jourdaines lay buried in the village of Beau Monde, France. Adrian is buried on La Quesnay ground with the rest of the family. Rod and I buried Journey and Jordan in our churchyard, together in the same box. She holds him forever," Tormond murmured.

"Does Reginald yet live?" Ruffian asked. Tessa became concerned when she saw the muscle in his jaw begin to twitch.

"Aye, he lives," Tormond answered, "But I hear tell he is not well. His greed and foolish ways have run the Barony to near ruin. Men still loyal to Adrian inform me that he babbles through the night and wanders the corridors in darkness. Some say he has a demon, others swear it's just too much ale. Reginald could never find the bounty Adrian had left for his heirs. He has employed soothsayers and psychics to reveal the gold's location, but to no avail. He always was a sore loser, even as a child. He always wanted what his brother had. Adrian had sent his entire fortune here to Sedgemoor as soon as he learned he was to become a father. He must've known Reginald would make an attempt to gain the title for himself, by any means possible. I was Adrian's insurance against that," Tormond added.

"So, we ride to Quesnay," Ruffian stated.

"Aye, son. We ride indeed."

There were plans to be made before the day of reckoning at Quesnay castle. Ruffian would ready the men himself. Rod saw to supplies and the horses. Tormond dispatched a missive to Edward II outlining the sordid tale of Reginald's antics. Ruffian would need to be recognized by both the Crown and the Church in order to usurp his Uncle. Edward despised Reginald's weak and simpering manner, thinking him an imbecile, so Tormond knew it wouldn't be difficult to gain the Crown's favor. The Church was only concerned with decorum, not morality one way or another. The parchment proved Ruffian was born of married parents and that he was christened the day after his birth.

They would be all the proof needed. *The rest will be child's play.* Tormond smiled. He had waited for this day for a very long time.

Ruffian followed Tormond through the maze of greying stones that surrounded the old chapel behind the keep. *My own mother was right under my nose the whole time,* Ruffian muttered and shook his head in frustration. Tormond sighed, "By the time you were old enough to handle the truth, their grave had grown over and blended in with the rest." He stopped before a stone made from a solid piece of rose quartz. After clearing the growth away, they both admired the way the stone shimmered in the sunlight.

"It shines the way she did, son," Tormond whispered.

Ruffian ran his hand across the gryphon gracing the top of the stone. The La Quesnay motto was inscribed there, in French. But below all that, were the words Ruffian hungered to read. *Journey Jourdaine La Quesnay and her son, Jordan lie in the arms of Christ the Lord.* Carved around the words were tiny rosebuds and thorns to symbolize the bitter-sweetness of life. Ruffian knew by the work on the stone that Tormond had spared no expense. His loyalty to his friends was true. Indeed, it had carried on, evident in his love for their son.

They continued to prepare for their mission. But oh, how they needed a day away. Tormond could see that look in her eyes again. The Lady of the keep needed time with her husband.

"Your cloak, Elspeth."

"Where are we going?"

"Away."

"But there's so much to do before you leave. We just can't scamper off to heaven knows where!" She slapped his hand away.

"Am I not the Lord of this keep?" he boomed in false fierceness.

"Aye, but…"

"You know," he grinned, "women are openly flogged in the courtyards of many a keep for defying their husbands. Do you wish to be chastised thusly?" His eyebrow cocked questioningly.

"Nay, M'lord, I do not wish to be beaten in the courtyard," she smiled.

"I should hope not! Now, your cloak, m'lady." He kissed her deeply, for the first time in ages, it seemed. They *would* have this one day together.

They set out for their special place. It was where the three rivers married into one. The rivers Vesica, Caerdroria, and Artress converged just to the north of the castle. Though the forest was rather daunting to most, Tormond knew the land well. Old legends bespoke of magic upon the place of the water's union. The *convergence* kept most people away. He knew they'd be alone there. The sun was high in the sky by the time they arrived. One whole day to be alone with his wife, his heart and soul.

Elspeth fanned out the MacLeod tartan blanket upon the grass. The MacLures were a sept of the Clan MacLeod and as such, donned the clan's colours. The MacLures had historically been the bards, poets, healers and musicians of the clan. The deep green, blue, black and gold, touched with a few scarlet threads held great meaning for the MacLeod Clan. *Jolie had done such beautiful work weaving it,* Elspeth thought as she smoothed the folds of wool. Tormond produced a leather pack filled with only the finest from the kitchens at Sedgemoor. The sound of softly flowing waters surrounded them as the Laird knelt before his Lady. She looked into his eyes and saw pure adoration there. He absolutely cherished her, and she knew it. He lifted the hem of her gown slightly and slipped off her shoes. She blushed like she was sixteen again. *She hasn't changed a bit from the day we met,* he smiled. He took her hand and led her down to the blanket. The ground was warm and welcoming as she lay there. The trees above them cast a filigree of light and shadow upon them as they held each other. The sun filtered through the leaves in sparkling motion. Breathing deeply, they fell into rhythm with one another; one breath—one heartbeat. He interlaced his fingers with hers and closed his eyes. *Life was so good.* Elspeth was a woman ahead of her time. She was one of the strongest people that Tormond had ever met. She was his guiding light; his grounding force that he needed. He knew the day they had first met that she alone would be the Lady of the keep.

The work carried on at Sedgemoor. By then, the truth of Ruffian's identity was known by all that lived there. He was a bit taken aback when the servants began to call him "m'lord" instead of his name. *I suppose I should get used to it, but it's all still so surreal,* he thought. He worked Tormond's men hard on the practice field. He wanted no mistakes, no mishaps when they took Quesnay. He wanted to keep the bloodshed to a minimum, after all, their 'enemies' would actually be the ones defending *his* castle.

The evening meal came and went with no sign of the MacLures. Tessa and Ruffian ate dinner with Jolie and Rod at the cottage. Ethan inhaled his food then left to tend the horses. Little Sarah, Jolie's daughter, had always adored Tessa. She played with the pendant around Tessa's neck.

"Ooh…it glows in the firelight!" Sarah marveled.

"Yes, it is a very special necklace. Your brother gave it to me as a gift."

"Some say he is not my brother, really."

"What do you think about that?"

"Well, it doesn't matter to me who he really belongs to. He's like my cat, Madelyn."

"He is?" Tessa was a little confused by the girl's logic.

"She was lost and needed a mommy. So I took her in," Sarah smiled, "She loves me even though I'm not a cat. Love doesn't care about things like that."

"You are right, Sarah. Do you know, you are very wise for your age?" Tessa hugged the little girl on her lap.

"Papa says I'm just like Mommy. I sometimes have fanciful thoughts."

"I think he's right."

"Sorry to intrude on this girl-talk," Ruffian interrupted, "But can I steal Tessa from you for a little while, Sarah?"

"Can she come back and play tomorrow?" They could tell by Sarah's tone that this was a deal-breaker.

"Of course, I'll come back tomorrow. We could ride to the oak if you like and I can tell you stories there," Tessa promised the girl.

"I shall be ready early," Sarah informed them, before scampering off to help Jolie clear their modest table.

The night air was cool for June, but it felt good to get out of the stuffy cottage. Ruffian took her hand and led her to the abbey. He pushed open the gate and pulled her inside. Shutting the iron gate behind them, he effectively shut out the rest of the world, at least for awhile. Hand in hand, they walked the stone paths they had walked as children. The garden hadn't changed much since then. The trees were taller and the boxwood had matured. Roses abounded everywhere.

"I think I missed this place the most when I was away," Ruffian sighed. He looked up through the roof that never was and watched the stars travel on their never ending journey.

"Why do you suppose the abbey was never finished?" he asked Tessa.

"There are stories, but I don't think anyone knows for certain. I had heard once that the people who lived here just disappeared one night. The townsfolk called it magic. But you can tell by this place that they worshipped God, not the ancient pagan ways," Tessa said.

"Where would they have gone? I mean, this place is fertile; surely they weren't without food. Do you think a pox fell upon them and they all died?"

"Nay, there would be graves here near the abbey."

"It is curious," Ruffian agreed, "I can't imagine why they would flee such a beautiful spot in Dundrennan."

"Father said the MacLures built here because of the springs that run underground. One actually feeds into to lowest level of the keep. Even if we befell a siege, we'd never run out of fresh water. The other reason was that my Great Grandfather swore his father had been drawn to this place. He saw the ruins of a previous dwelling and the abbey, of course. The remnants sat upon this grand hillside, so close to the sea. He was convinced that he was to build on this site. He called it 'The hand of God.' I cannot imagine growing up anywhere else."

Tessa climbed the spiraling stone staircase as far as it would lead. She reached up and traced the odd words carved into the stone. *Le tonnerre roule autour du trone.*

"Thunder rolls around the throne?" she asked Ruffian, "Edward's throne?"

"Nay, this is a century old, Tessa."

"God's throne?" she mumbled.

"That makes more sense, since it's an abbey we are standing in," he nodded as he looked around for more evidence.

"What happened to these people? Tessa was bothered by the mystery somehow.

"I don't know. I do know we aren't going to find the answers tonight," he said as he took her hand and led her down the steps.

"You're going to catch a chill," he murmured into her ear as he pulled her cloak tighter around her shoulders. His hands rested there and she leaned back against his chest. They both looked up to the night sky and were quiet for a time. Nature had a music all its own to entrance them.

"Tessa," he whispered. His velvet voice so close to her ear nearly made her dizzy. She could feel his breath upon her neck. He moved her hair aside and kissed her softly just behind her earlobe, "When shall we be together, love?"

"I wish it could be tonight, but this ring upon my finger bespeaks of my vow to wait, you know that," she smiled. She turned in his arms and looked up through her dark lashes in a most innocent way.

"Mark me, once I have Quesnay, I shall have you too."

"How long do you think you'll be gone?" she asked, *I don't think I can stand another six month separation.*

Ruffian studied the path of inlaid stone on the abbey floor. The prayer labyrinth could still be seen, though nature was slowly reclaiming it. He had no answer for Tessa's question. *How can I foresee how long it will take,* he thought.

"I will come back to you. When the castle is mine and my Uncle is gone, only then will I feel safe to have you by my side."

"I'm scared for you," she admitted, "I have a bad feeling about this."

"Reginald is weak. He's a drunkard and some say he's insane. I doubt very much he'll be a problem to contend with." Ruffian's usual cockiness came shining through. He wanted to put her at ease, though in truth, he was a bit nervous himself. The effects from the last battle he'd fought had not yet worn off. He still saw those eyes looking up at him in his dreams.

"Where is the leather tie I returned to you?" he asked as they made their way back to the keep, "I gave it back out of chivalry, and you never wear it anymore."

"I keep it in the box, with the other gifts."

"Why? It was yours to begin with."

"I keep everything you've given me in a very safe place," Tessa said, "It sits alone in a special place, holding many thoughts, smiles and intriguing memories. Some have even given me a glimmer of hope. Indeed, it holds concealed passions bound by duty, yet ever looking forward, even listening for the slightest sound that might announce a turning of a key in its locked haven." She smiled at the look on his face.

"I had no idea my gifts meant so much to you," Ruffian murmured.

"Aye, *m'lord*, there is much you do not yet know of me." Tessa's eyes held the promise of the coming years together. Ruffian wanted them to begin immediately.

CHAPTER 10

❀

THICKER THAN WATER

Amid the smokey light of early dawn, the men made ready to leave Sedgemoor. The horses snorted and stomped at the ground impatiently as they waited. Ruffian and Rod led their horses to the group. Everything had been checked and re-checked. Laird MacLure himself would accompany them to Quesnay for the reckoning. An old light rekindled in Tormond's eyes. *That sniveling coward will finally get what he deserves,* he assured himself as he adjusted the pack on his horse.

Rod had said his good-byes to Jolie and Serrah at the cottage. Ruffian had met with his mother the night before. Jolie now watched the gathering from her window at the weaving house. She watched as Elspeth and Tessa approached the men. With one more whispered prayer, the weaver turned her attention to the tapestry on her loom.

"Let's go already," Ethan said to a few other men.
"Easy son, don't be so anxious for the fight," Rod advised.

Tessa kissed her father's cheek and hugged him tightly.
"I love you. Thank you for all you have done on our behalf. I'm sorry there has been so much turmoil," she said.
"Someday, my darling girl, when you will have children of your own and you'll understand. It's never been a sacrifice to guard and raise you. I have

always considered it a privilege," Tormond whispered in her ear. His words crashed through her resolve and she lost the battle with the unshed tears that had been threatening since the night before.

"May I have a few words with Tessa before we leave?" Ruffian knew it was time to go.

"By all means." Tormond nodded and turned his full attention to his wife.

They had only walked a few feet when Tessa clamped her arms around his neck. She held him as tight as she could until he told her in a strangled voice, "Release me, wench. If I'm never allowed to leave, I shant be able to secure *your new home*."

"We can live in a hovel, if it means you won't go."

"I have to go, Tessa."

"I know you do," she sniffled, "Here, take this with you." She pulled the soft leather tie from her hair and handed it to him. Her hair fell down around her shoulders in auburn waves. He longed to be lost within them. *Soon, very soon,* he promised himself as the ram's horn was blown to signify their departure.

"I love you, Tessa. No matter what, don't ever forget," he said.

"I have always loved you. I will be here waiting." Her reply was lost in his kiss.

"Ahem, do the words 'get a chamber' mean anything to you?" Ethan smirked. "Can't this wait 'til the wedding night? We have an enemy to destroy and castle to claim, or are you so smitten you've forgotten?" Ruffian ignored his brother's teasing and kissed Tessa one last time.

"We *will* be together, mark my words."

The company of men rode out flying both the La Quesnay and MacLure banners. "Reginald's spotters will surely alert him of our approach, but the La Quesnay banner may gain us a few more yards. It will be a surprise, nevertheless," Tormond told Rod as they followed the old stone wall that meandered through the countryside, "The baron may be more than a little confused. After all, how many years has he sat as lord over Quesnay without dispute? Why even the Crown knew not of another living heir to the barony, though Edward surely knows by now. Nay, Reginald will never guess who is paying him a little visit."

Tessa watched from her tower window until she could see the men no longer. She snuffled back her tears in a most unladylike fashion, then flopped upon her bed for a full day of moping. She grabbed her feather pillow to smush it into a more comforting shape, when she felt a letter tucked underneath it. She smiled even before looking at it. Her baron had left her one more note before leaving. *He surely has no problem sneaking into my chambers,* she thought as she carefully broke the wax seal. She tried to pretend that he'd only be away a few days, but she knew it wouldn't be that simple. *Reginald has proven he is lethal. He's got too much to lose. He won't give up without a fight. Most likely, Adrian's parents died by Reginald's hand. We know what he did to Journey and Ruffian's brother. We also know he killed Adrian outright the night of All Hallows Eve. He'd kill Ruffian merely for the pleasure of it. And what about father? I'd never be able to face mother again if anything happened to him.* Her mind reeled. Her head was pounding. She decided to read his letter in the garden maze. Nowhere was she more at ease within herself, than in the abbey. She followed the spiraling path and made her way to the center. Reading his words to her in his bold sweeping script, she could almost hear his voice on the wind.

ᘯ

My Sweet Contessa,

Know this, that our parting is killing me. In all honesty, I cannot say how long this battle will take. The fight will be a hard one. You know as well as I do, that there is always a chance I may not return. I give you my oath that I will do everything in my power to see that does not occur. I pledge also to protect your father at all costs. Please tell your mother of this, I would have her know it.

If the Lord allows us success on our quest, the barony will be ours. I will send a runner with news as soon as it is safe to do so. Reginald's men will be given a chance to pledge their allegiance to me or to depart unharmed, from Quesnay land. As of now, I am truly uncertain how I will deal with my Uncle. I know I should let mercy lead, but meeting him face to face; the man who destroyed my family, may change my mind.

Until you hear from me, do not sit in your chamber and mope. Tessa snorted in response. *Trust me, and in the providential hand of God to lead us to victory. I will return for you, to wed you (and bed you) as soon as I can. I miss you already, Tessa. You must know by now, you are everything to me.*

I have been tormented in my dreams these last few nights as we have prepared to leave. I never thought I'd be engaging in battle again so soon. I can honestly tell you I could have lived without it. Callum still haunts me, you know. Shall I ever be able to forgive myself for such a terrible mistake? I pray time will ease the pain of regret. If perchance calamity strikes, and I shall be no more, know that I love you above all else. Your name wouldst be that last word I utter. Time on earth is fleeting. Regardless of circumstances, we shall not be separated forever. You know as well as I, that love transcends both time and space, aye, it even transcends worlds. I will be with you always, whether seen or unseen.

Keep the faith, dear one.
Your Ruffian,

Baron Rapheal La Quesnay

The summer breeze swirled around her as she finished reading the letter. It threatened to rip the parchment from her hand, but Tessa held fast to Ruffian's words. The altar in the center of the abbey was supposed to be the place where believers surrendered all to God. She watched as the ashes from the incense danced and then were blown away. The breeze grew suddenly colder. Tessa knew things at Sedgemoor would never be the same again.

The week's ride to Quesnay had been tediously slow for Ruffian and Ethan alike. Leaving Sedgemoor, they headed northeast until they reached the village of Eastborne. The men were fed and the horses tended to. The plan was to approach the castle under the cover of darkness. Ruffian took a few rare moments alone to open the third and final parchment that had been contained in the box from the south tower. He sat down in the stable near Thunder and popped open the wax seal. The parchment crinkled as he unrolled yet another bit of his past.

To my dear child,

I can only imagine the twisted turn of events that has led you to read this missive. It means I am not there to guide you on. From the day I was told that you moved within your dear mother, I have prayed that you would have a blessed and happy life. I know not if you be boy or lass, but I know you shall be strong, upright, and true to the calling. For that is your legacy.

With that being said, I want you to know that I place my faith and trust in you, child. You will honor me by being a child of God and a warrior or the truth, no matter the cost. I place my blessings upon you, as I give you up to His will.

You have my eternal love.
Your father,

Baron Adrian Paul La Quesnay

Ruffian gently folded the letter and placed it inside his tunic. *You will be with me in this, father,* Ruffian whispered as he sat alone and contemplated his next move. After a day's rest, they approached Quesnay castle. Even in darkness, the place seemed eerily familiar to Ruffian. He *had* been conceived here...*Bah! More of Tessa's fanciful thinking rubbing off on me,* he thought.

The horses were tied a quarter mile from the keep. The men moved quietly through the wooded hills that surrounded Quesnay. Ethan reached for his spyglass,
"There looks to be no more than three or four men walking the battlements."
"They will be easy to take," one of their kinsmen scoffed.
"What about guards who roam the grounds?" Ethan asked.
"You are paranoid, Bardougne!" the man laughed as they moved forward.
"Better paranoid, than dead," Ruffian told his brother, "keep your wits about you and your eyes open, Ethan."
"Aye, m'lord."
"Would you cut that out?" Ruffian sighed.
"M'lord?" he grinned.
"Stop it!"
"Boys," Rod stepped in, "Now is not the time. Focus on our objectives, you can argue over titles later."
"Well said," Tormond nodded.

The predawn mist arose from the hills. It was the time to attack with optimum advantage. To be fair, they had carried both banners as they approached the keep. They, at least, still upheld the realm's rules of engagement. As they got closer, the men could see the few guards running back and forth among the battlements. Their lack of training showed, as some panicked and disappeared from view. *Something we will have to remedy,* Ruffian said to himself as he began to scale the north wall of greying stone.

Reginald La Quesnay snored on in blissful ignorance. His too-pale body lay slumped over a haggard chambermaid. He snorted and whistled most annoyingly in her ear. The room reeked of stale wine and old tobacco smoke. The fire had long since gone out in the hearth. The cold had begun to creep in from the small window above the bed. The cloth used in place of glass had worn away years ago. A frantic pounding on the door only partially roused the lord of the manor.

"Lord Reginald! We are being attacked! There must be hundreds, thousands of them! They carry your banner, m'lord, it is most distressing!" a belabored squire called to Reginald. He merely rolled over and snored on. The maid he had bedded gathered her meager clothing and slipped from the room. Reginald had little use for her in the morning light, and she wanted no part of the visitors who had come to Quesnay castle.

As Tormond and his men made a rather nasty ruckus outside, Ruffian entered the great hall. He found no one, except for a servant lad tending the fire. Ruffian stalked over to him, moving quietly in the darkness. He lifted the boy up by the tunic, eye to menacing eye.

"Where does your lord abed, boy?" he growled. The wide-eyed boy sputtered, but managed to choke out the way to Reginald's chambers. Taking the spiraling steps two at a time, Ruffian soon stood at the foot of his uncle's bed.

"Arise, toad."

"What infernal racket is this?" Reginald slurred.

"'Tis the day you pay for your crimes."

Not fully awake, Reginald struggled to make meaning of the intrusion. As his bleary eyes cleared, he moaned in exasperation.

"By the saints, brother! Will you *never* leave me in peace?" Ruffian cocked an eyebrow in amusement as his hand encircled his uncle's throat, and he began to tighten.

"Is that who you think I am?" Ruffian grinned wickedly as the man began to gag and cough.

"Tis you, I am sure of it, Adrian, for behold the ring you wear! Even in death, you keep it from me. You've not given me a moment's peace in all these years!" Reginald seemed almost perturbed. Imagine the gall of his dead brother, to bother him that way. *It's almost comical,* Ruffian smiled, *Tormond's men must have been correct about the reports of his rather fragile mental state.*

"Cease your prattling, old man," Ruffian ground out as he flung him back onto the knot of twisted sheets.

The steel of Ruffian's blade cut ever so slightly into Reginald's thick neck. He gulped as he felt the faint trickle of blood seep into his nightshirt.

"Look closer, baron. I am not Adrian. Do I not have the features of another you have known?" Ruffian increased his pressure on the blade.

"Stop it! Stop it!" Reginald moaned all the more, he held his hands to his ears as if to shut out the voices that resided there.

"Are you his dead son, then? You resemble the trollop he bred with. 'Twas not by my hand you met your end! She need not have run away like that. I'll not take on the sins of another!" he yelled.

"You need not take on other's sins, when the list of your own is so lengthy." Tormond walked into the chamber and looked at Reginald.

"You!" Reginald spat, "I should have known you'd be involved! Edward will have your head for this!"

"I daresay Edward will have yours first, possibly gift-wrapped and sent to him on a platter," Tormond said in a low voice. "Ethan has been wounded, son."

"Is it bad?"

"Bad enough, but he'll live," Tormond assured him. "He's being taken care of in the kitchens."

"Who are you then?" the bewildered man asked Ruffian, oblivious to Tormond's words.

"Look closely. I am the one you never counted on, Uncle. You see, Journey gave birth to *two* sons that October night."

"Oh my God. That's not true. They told me she had one and…"

"That she and the baby both died that night? Aye, they did indeed. But there was one twist no one expected, least of all you," Ruffian smiled.

"Another baby." Reginald couldn't believe his luck.

"I am a child no longer, and you dear Uncle, will surely rue the day you even so much as looked at my mother."

The great hall was filling with confused people by the time Ruffian and Tormond escorted Reginald to the landing. Their men had relieved the guards of their weapons with ease. Ruffian made a mental note; Quesnay castle would not be so easily taken once he became lord. He pushed Reginald closer to the railing overlooking the crowd.

"Hear me, good people. We mean you no harm. I seek only what is rightfully mine by virtue of my birth." The crowd began to murmur.

"Tell them the truth, Uncle, or as God as my witness, you will leap to your death here and now."

Reginald raised a trembling hand to quiet the crowd. He felt the tip of Ruffian's sword press harder against his back as he hesitated.

"Loyal people, I must confess I have many a misdeed in my past. For over twenty years I have served as your lord. I have done my best to take care of you, but it seems as if I came upon this title in error." The crowd began to whisper among themselves.

"The *truth*, Uncle." Ruffian pressed the blade yet again.

"My brother, Adrian was the first born, God rest his soul, and as such inherited the title over Quesnay. After his death, um...I took his place."

"What he's not telling you is that Adrian met his death by Reginald's hand!" Ruffian shouted.

"I am the son of Adrian La Quesnay. And as such, the title is mine alone. Now, you people have two choices, you can swear allegiance to me, Rapheal La Quesnay, or you can leave peacefully. I do not want bloodshed, but I will not hesitate to end any life that thinks to scheme against me any longer. That is a promise. You have until sunset to make your decision. From that point on, there will be no second chances."

"What are you going to do to me?" Reginald was almost scared to ask.

"I am going to make you tell your people what you have done to this family."

"I can't do that," he shook his still-throbbing head no.

"Confession is good for the soul, Reginald, and yours needs all the help it can get," Tormond assured him. Reginald began to sweat profusely as he fumbled for the words to explain his actions.

"I was young and foolish. I envied my brother's birthright. As a second son, I knew I would receive nothing in comparison. It wasn't fair! I had nothing against Adrian personally, I just let greed cloud my judgment," Reginald explained.

"Poor, misunderstood man. Go on," Ruffian commanded.

"Our sire was already terribly ill, so it was really a merciful thing I did putting him out of his misery. Our Lady mother was naught but in the way, with father gone. She had far too much time on her hands, always sticking her nose where it didn't belong. Her fall on the stairs was merely a fortunate coincidence! With both of them gone, I knew it was my *destiny* to rule over the house of Quesnay! 'Tis true! The voices told me so!" he added to prove his point. Ruffian whistled at how far-gone his uncle really was, and Rob merely rolled his eyes.

"Enough theatrics, old man, what about my parents?"

"It was all I could do not to murder Adrian outright when he announced his strumpet would deliver him a mongrel at harvest time!" The blade pressed again on his back.

"After mother's accident, there was quite a bit of tension hereabouts. Month's passed and things grew worse, I admit. I found myself thinking about Journey more and more. If I could just get Adrian out of the way, I thought Journey and I could be together. I tried being nice to her, I really did! But the whore wouldn't even acknowledge me! I lost control and threatened her one night, a stupid move, I know. Adrian sent her away to drop-calf elsewhere. 'Twas fine by me, I never wanted to see her face again! The more I thought about it, the more I wanted to take the one thing my brother valued above all else. Only two guards flanked her side as she left Quesnay. She'd be easily taken care of; my men assured me of it. She was never supposed to reach Sedgemoor alive."

The crowd was dead silent, wrapped up in the horror story Reginald was recounting. Tormond's men stood nearby and watched them. There would be no disruptions until the entire story had been confessed for all to hear.

"My men said they chased them for nigh unto a week. It was like an unseen force kept them from overtaking the wench and her guards. You must understand, I could not allow that child to live. He would've stood in the way of my destiny." Reginald's eyes were wild as he babbled on.

"My men arrived at Sedgemoor just as the whelp was born. They said she was covered in blood and both mother and child were dead. God took them both! I swear I had nothing to do with it. A runner was sent ahead of my men with the news I had been longing for. Unfortunately, Adrian had not lived to hear it. I so wanted him to grieve his dear family, but on the night of All Hallows Eve, he became a madman. He'd been drinking because he missed her so, and he came at me with his broadsword. We fought to the death. He lost. I won. I had won it all!" Reginald's voice broke as he fell in a heap on the floor.

The stunned crowd looked up collectively at Ruffian.

"What my uncle never knew is that my mother gave birth to twins that night at Sedgemoor. I stand before you as the rightful heir to Quesnay." Two men lifted the crumpled form off the floor to meet Ruffian's steely eyes.

"To kill you would indeed give me some measure of satisfaction. However, it would make me no better than you, I suppose." Ruffian paced as he weighed his options.

"Therefore, you shall live, provided you leave Quesnay immediately and forever. Hear me well, I choose to forgive you. This is not for your benefit, but my own. The killing has to stop. I choose to stop it here and now. The acts of your hand have severed forever any ties between us. There is nothing left for you here. You are no longer under La Quesnay protection. If you are ever spotted on this land again, you will be shot for trespassing. You will never hurt my family again. I pray God has mercy on your soul, because you will find no further mercy here." Ruffian turned and walked away.

CHAPTER 11

※

KINDRED SPIRITS

Aout 1309
Quesnay Castle

Reginald was none-too-gently escorted off La Quesnay land. Ruffian allowed him to take what personal belongings he desired, and a horse. He posted his men along Quesnay's borders for several weeks after Reginald's departure. Ethan was in charge of training the men of La Quesnay, better combat skills. With his arm wrapped tightly to his chest, he barked out orders as the men progressed through the drills. He loved the chance to boss others around. If Reginald planned retaliation, Ethan made sure that Ruffian would be ready and waiting. At night, Ethan would sit alone on the battlements and scan the sky with his spyglass. He thought he was dead when he sustained such a massive wound to his forearm. He closed his eyes and shuddered when he remembered the bone and muscle being laid bare. It was then that Ethan began making plans for his own path; his own life.

A runner was sent to Sedgemoor to inform the women of the news. Reginald was gone, and Quesnay was theirs. Ruffian asked Tessa to allow them a month to make the keep *livable* before they joined him there. Once the filth was removed and the rubbish hauled away, the keep was not in bad repair. The floors were cleared of molding rushes and rotting food. Fresh herbs and scented grasses were brought in and laid down. All the chambers were opened to air out. The stench of neglect slowly faded away. Tormond's men were well skilled in masonry and carpentry. They were happy to share their knowledge with the residents. Those who dwelled in the barony were so grateful to have a new and kinder lord, they poured themselves into a massive renovation. The work would continue through the summer and near to harvest time.

Jolie walked the shore of the river Artress in silence. The intricately braided silk cord around her waist boasted a set of aged keys that jingled as she walked. The rhythmic chimes were soothing. The sun was setting and her weaving was finished for the day. Serrah had talked Betsy, one of the chambermaids, into letting her spend the night in the keep. Jolie had some time to herself.

"Pleasant evening, my friend!" Atremis called from the opposite side of the river.

"Aye, sir, it is."

"You shouldn't be out here alone. I hope you weren't going to venture to the convergence."

"I thought you were a man of science, not superstition."

"Why tempt fate, my friend?" he smiled.

"There is no such thing as fate."

"Call it what you will, the forces here are bigger than you and I will ever know."

"That, we agree on. So, what are you doing out here tonight?" she asked as they both approached the arched, stone bridge that spanned the waters.

"I'm mapping."

"This land has been well mapped before," she cocked her eyebrow in amusement.

"Not the land. I'm tracking the sun, moon, and the five wanderers," he said.

"Of course. You have to keep an eye on those pesky wanderers." she smiled.

Artemis was a bit of a local legend. He was known by many names; in many different places. His given name was Artemesia, or *Silver King*. He was known by the name Owahseeah, on some of his more ominous travels. He lived across the river, among the standing stones at the Heathersage circles. He had built a tall stone dome that reached into the sky. He called it his observatory. It boasted odd windows in ridiculous locations, that Artemis used for his studies. His abode was filled with stacks of parchments and scrolls piled into baskets. Strange metal measuring devices sat on dusty shelves. He lived as a hermit and seemed to like it that way. He was the caretaker of the circles. Even in 1309, their original use was a mystery. Artemis swore they were calendars, marking the progression of the sun and seasons.

Jolie had met him while hunting mushrooms just after she arrived at Sedgemoor. He startled her at first, a tall man with his long silver hair braided and tied, carrying a basket upon his back filled with plants and parchments. He wore a long robe over his tunic and leggings, and his shoes were made of wool instead of leather. A vegetarian, he would never think of harming another living creature for food or clothing. He proved to be a kindly man as well as most intellectual. Jolie enjoyed their talks on philosophy and astronomy. He taught her about many medicinal plants that she'd never seen growing up in France. Though not a resident of Sedgemoor, he made himself available to the MacLures if the need arose. He was a wonderful healer and the caretaker of so many secrets locked within the Dundrennan hills. He challenged Jolie and made her look deeper for the answers that alluded her.

"How goes it with the work at Quesnay?" he asked as he slipped off his woolen shoes and splashed at the water's edge.

"From what we hear, all is well. Ethan was wounded when they took the castle, but Rod assures me he is healing. We shall join them next month. Would you like to come? It's been a long time since you've been there."

"You know I cannot," he said.

"Reginald is gone, my friend. The evil that you felt there has been swept away."

"I vowed I would never return there and I meant it. I'll stay here and look after things at home. I assume Lady Elspeth will go with you."

"Aye, she'll go. And no doubt she begin making changes to the manor before we even unpack," Jolie snorted.

"What's this? Is there a problem with you two?" He already knew the answer to his question. He knew more than Jolie could ever imagine about her relationship with Elspeth. The struggle had begun long ago. It became more pronounced upon Ruffian's birth. Artemis knew all about it, and understood the dynamic perfectly, though Jolie had no clue why Elspeth *irked* her so.

"She seems ill at ease with my relationship with Tessa. We are friends. She trusts me with things. Since I'm not her mother, I guess I can listen to her without judging her. That is something Elspeth finds difficult at times, I fear."

She's jealous," he stated, "You are 'mother' to Ruffian, a child she would've liked to have raised herself, and then you go and become friends with her only daughter. She feels threatened by you."

"Threatened? It's her keep! Believe me, she never lets me forget it!" Jolie fumed, "She sits in her grand tower and tries to control people and events to serve her own agenda."

"Why are you getting so upset?" he smiled.

"Because Ruffian is my son, not hers."

"Your son? You knew when you took him in that you would someday have to give him up to his own heritage." Artemis knew when to be loving but firm with her. She was not being logical.

"My head knows that, but my heart screams to hold onto him," she confessed.

"You can never lose Ruffian, not really. Another might have given birth to him, but you gave him a life. You kept him safe. You raised him well. Now you have to set him free. He will not depart from all you've taught him. In his heart, you and Rod *are* his parents. No one can take that away. Have you not seen the correlation? Elspeth feels the same way about Tessa." Jolie had never looked at it that way before. She grinned sheepishly.

"I shall speak with Elspeth before we leave."

"I knew you would," he smiled, "Now, would you like to come to the observatory for some fresh catnip tea? I gathered the honey myself! Or can I tempt you with some fennel? 'Tis good for digestion."

"Thank you, but no. I need to get back to the keep. Serrah is running amuck with Betsy. I think it's best that I check on her before going to bed."

"Be at ease, my friend," he said as he slipped his shoes on and headed back toward Heathersage. She watched him disappear into the wooded hillside. She had turned and began walking to the keep when someone whispered her name.

"Jolie Essex."

"What?" she spun on her heel and pulled a dagger from her belt in one fluid motion. "Who are you? Come from the shadows and make thyself known to me." She'd not been called that name in years. A darkly clad figure stepped from the tree line that gently hugged the river. She backed up a few steps.

"You are Jolie Essex, are you not?" he asked.

"My name is Bardougne now," she eyed him with suspicion. "What business have you with me?"

"Blessings from the Holy One, I am Michael. You know my brethren, Phillip and Nicholas, do you not?" he asked.

"You are one of the 33?" She breathed a sigh of relief, for if Michael was one of the brotherhood, she knew she had nothing to fear from him.

"Nay, the 33 you of which speak does not exist. They are nothing more than legend and myth," he smiled gently. The hood of his cloak cast a shadow over his face. Jolie could only see the hint of wavy brown hair that refused to stay neatly tucked away. He had a strong chin and trimmed mustache and goatee. She saw a small earring flash with the last rays of the setting sun.

"Have you word from Nicholas?" she asked, still unsure what this man wanted with her.

"Both he and Phillip are well. They are in Brittany as we speak, tending to a small disturbance there."

"Really." Jolie knew only enough of the 33 to know that no 'disturbance' was small, and that the instigators rarely lived long enough to repent of their deeds.

"I have word from Cressex," Michael said as he handed Jolie a leather bundle tied with sinew. Jolie noticed the ring he wore on his left hand; a knotwork band with an opal imbedded into the setting. Phillip and Nicholas wore the same. Michael was who he said he was, or it was a very elaborate hoax.

Jolie felt uneasy as soon as she took the bundle into her hands. She untied the knot and lay open the leather. A finely polished horn chalice slipped from the soft doeskin.

"This belongs to Chelsea...what happened?" she looked to Michael.

"Cressex has fallen to the pox."

"She's dead?" Jolie felt her head begin to spin and her stomach lurch.

"The village is no more. I was there at the worst of it. We did all we could, but it was too late. I tended to Chelsea myself. She gave me this and swore me to promise I'd get it to you somehow."

"We made this cup while on the weaver's solstice just last harvest," she said as she caressed the smooth horn. "It was one of the tasks I required of my students as we journeyed through the solstice. I had Rod craft the iron holder before I ventured to our meeting spot. After Chelsea finished the horn, I gave her the holder as a gift. She was so proud of it." The horn was smooth and polished, it nested in the iron cradle perfectly.

"It was important to her that you have it," Michael whispered.

"The pox?" she said as she dropped the chalice and stepped back.

"It is clean. I made sure before leaving the village that I took nothing defiled with me."

"Are the children gone too?"

"I regret to tell you, all have fallen." Michael looked grim. "Be assured, she was at peace at the end. She wanted you to know she loved you."

Jolie picked up the chalice and carefully re-wrapped it in the skin. She wiped her face with her sleeve, and turned to thank Michael for his kindness. He had vanished as quietly as he had appeared. This was common for those of the 33 messengers, as they attended to their duties throughout the land. Like an unseen force, they watched over those of faith within the realm.

Tessa decided she would not give in to her emotions. She missed Ruffian, but life could not stop without him there. They would be together soon, though she felt not soon enough. Since she was not quite the domestic type, she spent her time reading to Serrah beneath the oak, or training with Sir Stanton behind the keep. Stanton was a member of a contingent of men commanded to stay behind and guard Sedgemoor and the family while Tormond was away. Tessa had a way of bending him to her will. She always wanted the same thing; an hour or two on the practice field. He used to baby her, but she made him pay dearly for such kindness. Once, she opened his leggings from waist to crotch with the tip of her blade in one smooth motion. From then on, he showed her no mercy, which is exactly what she wanted. Training was a waist, without a truly worthy opponent. The events of the world surrounding her were beyond her control, but on the field she had complete control. It was her strength, her agility, her training and self-discipline that carried her through. The nights were the hardest. Tessa tried to make herself so exhausted that she would just fall asleep after supper, but now and then, she was painfully aware of how alone she was without him.

Weeks went by, as they prepared to journey to Quesnay. Elspeth was kept busy by both packing linens and personal items for the trip, as well as making sure her own household would be in order while she was away. It was almost harvest time. They had few men to spare at Sedgemoor. Rod returned with ten men to accompany the ladies. Jolie had also heard from her friends, Nicholas and Phillip, who would also be traveling with them. They filled the wagons with foodstuffs and spices, linens and silks and tapestries to adorn Tessa's new home. Jolie worked closely with Artemis, procuring as many medicinal herbs as she could. It seemed all was ready.

"May I speak with you, m'lady?" Jolie asked Elspeth in the hall, late one evening.

"Oh, Jolie, I wanted to ask you if you think we have packed enough bed coverings?"

"Ah…yes, I believe so. If it wouldn't be too much trouble, could we sit and talk for a moment?"

"Of course, what's wrong?" Elspeth's brow furrowed. Jolie could tell she was still mentally ticking things off her things-to-do list.

"I want to apologize if I have ever over-stepped my bounds with lady Tessa."

"I don't understand." Elspeth looked lost at the topic of conversation.

"Tessa. I'm sorry if my friendship with her has been unseemly in any way."

"As far as I can tell, you've done nothing wrong, Jolie. What is this really about?" Elspeth asked quietly. The flames flickered in the hearth as both women felt some sort of huge weight upon them. Neither quite knew how to address it. They weren't enemies. Jolie had served them well, since the day Rod had brought her there from France as his bride. But they weren't friends either. Of course, being separated by social class made friendship difficult, but it had never been a problem for Tormond and Rod. It was something else that kept them distant.

"I just wanted to confront any issues we might have had with one another before leaving," Jolie said. "I don't want to add any more unrest to that place, after Ruffian has worked so hard to bring about healing."

"It is God who heals."

"Yes, and sometimes He uses good men to do it."

"None are good, in and of themselves. 'Tis the Lord who is good," Elspeth murmured. Jolie began to feel that old feeling of exasperation, *must every conversation be this way?*

"Goodnight m'lady," she said as she bobbed and left the hall.

Tessa walked into the hall and found her mother mumbling something as she worked a knotted piece of needlepoint in the firelight.

"Mother?"

"That woman! Was she sent her to test me? By the saints, she is the bane of my existence," Elspeth continued to mumble. Tessa couldn't follow it though, because of the thread tightly pinched between her mother's lips.

"Jolie?"

"How did you know?" Elspeth asked,

"Mother! Are you blind? Can you not see how alike you are? 'Tis comical to watch you both!" Tessa laughed outright. Elspeth looked horrified at the thought.

"What do you mean we are alike? I am nothing like her!" she screeched.

"Yes you are. Like right now! I bet if I was talking to Jolie, she say the same thing of you!" Tessa smiled.

"She'd see 20 lashes for it too!" Elspeth huffed.

"Aye, and *that's* the difference. You have all the power, mother. Can you imagine what it's like not to be able to voice your thoughts and feelings? You both are such strong women, but *you* will always have the upper hand.

"Am I to apologize for that?"

"No, you are to understand that, and maybe try to show respect for the person Jolie truly is." Tessa kissed her mother on her cheek, "Goodnight, mother. I love you."

"I love you too, dear." Elspeth suddenly felt exhausted. She really did admire Jolie for all her talents and strengths. In fact, she knew deep down her feelings stemmed from fear. Jolie had a knack with her own children and Elspeth's children as well. She was truly friendly with men and women alike. Social standing was not an issue. It was an easiness Elspeth had never been able to master. Jolie seemed to be a younger, freer version of Elspeth, and she resented her for it. It was something she needed to settle in her own heart and mind.

The next morning, everyone at Sedgemoor assembled to say goodbye. The staff assured Elspeth *several times* that they had everything well in hand. Tessa and her mother would ride in the MacLure carriage alone. The Bardougnes, including Serrah, would follow them. Brendan and Phillip each accompanied a carriage, while the rest of Tormond's men kept a keen watch for bandits or wild animals. The procession was an impressive one. Tessa smiled when it ironically reminded her of the Stolford's arrival at Sedgemoor some month's back. Would those at Quesnay welcome her there?

He hadn't even attempted to sleep. Five days and counting; Tessa would be there soon. Ruffian walked the hallways of the keep thinking of her; that's of course when he wasn't up on the battlements, driving the guards crazy. All at the castle were eagerly awaiting the arrival of the new Lady La Quesnay.

"He needs a stiff drink," Rod ventured to say as he watched his son pace.

"I daresay he needs something a bit more *comforting*," Ethan laughed.

"Time enough for that, son, after the nuptials."

"How long have you been in love with mother? Did you know her long before your marriage?"

"Hmmm, let me think. It has been awhile ago, you know," Rod smiled, "I had returned to the village of Brionne, France, to visit family there. As I recall, I was seventeen. I'd been working at Sedgemoor since I was a lad, and I had finally been promoted to stable master. I thought instead of sending the money home to my parents, I'd bring it to them in person, and have a short visit. I arrived just in time for some sort of village celebration of the spring. All the people had gathered at the river Risle to picnic and to enjoy the sunshine. I remember seeing the sun glinting off her hair. She was sitting with friends on an azure blue blanket 'neath a copse of birch trees. The breeze was combing through her tresses as she laughed with the other girls," Rod recalled in fine detail.

"Love at first sight?" Ethan mused.

"Nay, maybe for me, but not for your mother. My sister, Aimee, was among her group of friends. She spotted me and called me over to the group. Jolie wouldn't give me the time of day. I thought her a most beautiful *snob*. But later, as I sat eating a meal with my parents, I caught her looking at me. When I met her stare, her face turned a bright red and she disappeared into the crowd. Your mother has always liked to think she hides her emotions well, but we both know she is miserable at facades."

"Aye, isn't it the truth!" Ethan smirked and shook his head.

"I found her later. She was alone this time, walking the path leading to the kissing stone."

"The what?"

"What, what? Oh, the kissing stone? It was a boulder in the middle of Mont-claire Forest. No one knows how it got there, for there are no others like it around for miles. Anyway, 'tis said whoever has their first kiss while sitting upon the kissing stone, will one day marry. It was said to be a most blessed spot. Generations of my people *swore* by the kissing stone."

"So why was she headed that way alone?"

"Consequently, her family's farm lay through those woods. She was merely on her way home. *So she says*," Rod grinned.

"You think she was leading you there?" Ethan's eyes widened.

"I cannot say for sure. Mayhap the stone was leading us both there that evening. But I knew I could not return to Sedgemoor without at least talking to her. I saw her disappear into the tree line of the woods. I knew the path well from my boyhood. So, I followed the wench into the forest. By the time I entered the brambles and undergrowth, I couldn't see her ahead of me. I could only hear her singing as she went. The paths had changed since my childhood, after all, I *had* been away for a very long time. I got myself turned around and with the sun quickly setting, I knew I would soon be in a bit of trouble. I could still hear her in front of me somewhere, so though it galled me to do it; I called out to her."

"You didn't?"

"I know, I know, how humiliating!" Rod laughed. "At first she didn't respond. I thought I had frightened her. Then I heard her laugh. Like the chimes in the breeze, her laughter was. She bid me to identify myself and I did so. Again, I heard no response. I called out to her, but this time I was beginning to get perturbed. She laughed and bade me to admit I was a bumbling fool who could not find my way out of a privy. I did so, for a man knows when to concede defeat. Then a hand reached out and grabbed my shoulder from behind. I nearly wet myself in the surprise of it!"

"Now *that* would've been embarrassing!" Ethan hooted as he looked out across the moonlit hills.

"It wouldn't have mattered at that point, son. She already thought me a complete idiot. She smiled at me with pity as if I was a poor half-drowned kitten being pulled from a well. She led me by the hand back to the trail and we came upon the kissing stone. We sat for a moment to rest. I don't think she realized that I knew where we were. I reached over and took her hands in mine. She tried to pull free but I held tight and stole a kiss."

"Without permission? You stole a kiss?"

"Well, I stole *the first one.* The others were given most freely, I assure you." Rod winked at his son. "I knew I had to sway her quickly because my visit was going to be a short one. I courted her for the next fortnight and then asked her to marry. She was sixteen then. Her father was more than willing, even though he knew it meant she would come to live with me at Sedgemoor. Robert Celestine was a very dynamic man. He convinced her she would be happy with me. Jolie trusted his judgment and we married the day before I was to leave. Just a few months later, we were given Ruffian to raise, and then Jolie found out she was carrying you. We've had a very good life together. It's never been boring, I'll give you that much."

"Looks like Ruffian has finally gone to bed," Ethan said.

"Well then, we shall too. Goodnight, son."

"Good sleeping, father," Ethan said as he watched Rod step into the castle.

Ethan began to look back at his life, and the truth be told, he was less than impressed by it. He was a year younger than Ruffian, but what adventures had he had? Yes, he had seen battle. He almost watched his brother die on the field that day. His own wound there at Quesnay reminded him again of all that he had not yet accomplished. He could've died, and what had he done that people would remember him by? Nothing. He had never traveled beyond the battle-fields. He'd never seen France, his ancestral homeland. He'd never known a woman, or real love. Tessa and Ruffian would be staying on at Quesnay, so who would be left at Sedgemoor? *Family is important,* he thought, *but there comes a time to step out on one's own.* The thought continued to dance around his mind as he too, attempted to get some sleep. *Surely, Tessa would arrive by morning.*

CHAPTER 12

※

TRINITY

Septembre 1309
Quesnay Manor

"Open the gate!" Ruffian commanded as he climbed the stairway to the gatehouse.

"Aye, m'lord, but there's still no sign of yer Lady," the sentry offered.

"She'll be here today, I know it." The sentry did as he was told, but rolled his eyes at the other guard when Ruffian turned his back.

"That's what he's said these past two days," he mumbled.

Quesnay Manor loomed largely over the rolling countryside. The trees had just begun to turn with explosions of rich jeweled colors. The grass was still lush and green along the road leading up to the manor. Late summer flowers dotted the hills as the carriages made their way through the land. Bright banners snapped and waved from every tower, in welcome. The House of La Quesnay was ready to greet its Lady. Of course it wasn't official yet, since there had been no wedding, but Tessa would be looked on as the Lady of the manor regardless. After the long line of strumpets Reginald had paraded in front of his people, Tessa would be a most welcome improvement.

Tessa could see the castle from miles away. She stuck her head out the carriage window and took in her surroundings. *It's huge! How am I ever going to manage a household of that size?* she thought. Her head began to ache.

"You'll be fine, Tessa," Elspeth said, "I'm sure they have a full staff to help you."

"I hate it when you do that, mother," Tessa laughed.

"I can't help it. Besides, I felt the exact same way just before I entered Sedgemoor for the first time." She settled back in the carriage as they made their way around the curving road leading to the keep. It would be a day she'd never forget. She knew Ruffian was waiting for her.

"Carriages approach, m'lord," the sentry called.

"How many?" Ruffian asked as he and Ethan reached the battlements.

"Here, use this," Ethan elbowed his brother. Ruffian took the spyglass Ethan offered. Finding it hard to track a moving target, he finally was able to catch a glimpse of Tessa in the larger of the two coaches. She was laughing at something. Her cheeks were pink from the early autumn air. Her hair was loose around her shoulders. Ruffian handed the glass back to his brother and headed for the stairway.

"Brother, are you not the *Baron* now?" Ethan laughed.

"So?"

"So, that means that you let *her* come to *you*."

"You're an idiot, Ethan."

"Bah! I assure you, I will never traipse around like a lovesick puppy after *my* woman!"

"What woman?" Ruffian smirked, "The only wench I've ever seen you so much as dance with was Lillie, that buck-toothed girl from the creamery."

"She was an excellent dancer!" Ethan protested.

"Aye, like a one legged bar wench at a rat stomp?"

"Besides, after the dance, she gave me a peek under her skirts."

"You lie."

"On my honor, she did! But truth be told, her torn stockings and droopy woolen bloomers were a rather scary site. I ventured no further!"

"Ethan, I wonder what you will do without me there to guide you along?" Ruffian slapped his brother on the back.

"I don't know what I'll do, honestly." Ethan was suddenly serious.

"You could stay on here. I need you to work with these men. I'm sure Tessa could find a willing wench for you."

"Thanks, but no. I was thinking of doing some traveling; some exploring on my own."

"Mother will throw a holy fit!"

"She'll get over it. She's letting you go, isn't she? After all, she'll still have Serrah at home. I venture to guess in a few years, that one will be a hand full!"

"Poor father; alone in the house with those two!" Ruffian mused. The brothers caught sight of Rod as they crossed the bailey. When he looked at them in confusion, they both burst out laughing.

Tessa sat back in her seat as they entered the bailey yard. Her stomach felt the way it always did when she knew she must have a visit from the physician; nervous and nauseous at the same time. It had been nearly two months since she had seen Ruffian's face. He would be different somehow, changed by his newly found position. She glanced hesitantly out the carriage window and saw him there. He looked fit and healthy. He was tanned and the work on the keep had built up the muscles in his arms even more than before. She suddenly felt very warm. A bead of sweat gently trickled down between her breasts.

"Tessa!" Elspeth shouted, "I asked if you were ready to go?"

"Aye, mother, I'm ready." She took a deep breath and closed her eyes; slowly letting the air escaped through her parted lips. Her head was spinning. Tormond was already at the carriage door. He lifted Elspeth out and into his warm embrace.

"It's been too long, love," he whispered into Elspeth's hair. A moment later, he was there. Ruffian offered his hand, but Tessa sat still.

"M'lady?"

"Aye."

"Would you care to get out of this god-forsaken hay wagon, or do you want me to come in there after you?" He grinned. He reached out and touched her hand. She was shaking.

"Tessa?"

"Aye."

"Come to me, Tess. I've missed you so." She slowly took his hand. His fingers entwined themselves with hers. He noticed her hands were clammy. He helped her down and wrapped her black cloak just a bit tighter around her shoulders. The people of Quesnay wanted to get a good look at her, but Ruffian quickly took her in his arms and whisked her into the keep. He gently kissed her forehead, then frowned.

"You feel warm."

Rod collected Serrah and Jolie from the second carriage. Ethan picked Serrah up and boasted her on his one good shoulder as they entered the keep.

"Darlin' girl, you are a sight for these weary eyes," Rod said.

"You sound like an old man."

"I am old, and feelin' older by the day without you here."

"You're only forty-three, Rod."

"Aye, my papa died at forty," he sighed.

"You're not dying."

"I fear I shall, if you don't kiss me now, wench," he winked. Jolie reached up and gathered him into her arms. She combed her fingers through his soft brown hair as she gave her mouth fully to his. Their tongues; in pursuit of each other, soon gave way to a rhythmic dance of liquid warmth perfected by years of faithfulness.

"Do you still feel old?" she asked as she ended the kiss. Her brown eyes were sparkling. Rod pressed himself closer to her as he held her; his hand gently lingering on the small of her back.

"What do *you* think?" he asked.

"I think, Roderick Bardougne, that you'd best show me to our quarters, so we can find out."

❦   ❦   ❦

"How did you happen upon this place, friend?" the hooded one asked quietly as he warmed his beautiful hands over the fire.

"Erlick the Red is a friend from my boyhood. I was told long ago that if I was ever in need of, ah…sanctuary, to come here. I must say though, Trascrow isn't as grand as I remember it," Reginald said as he looked around the rat-infested keep.

"Erlick is a faithful servant of the church, as I hear you are, Baron La Quesnay."

"Bah! The Barony be damned. In truth, I'm glad to be free of it," he lied.

"Truly? Then you'd not be interested if I were to tell you of a way to reinstate you as lord?" the monk smiled.

"There is no such way," Reginald hissed.

"We take care of our own. It has come to the Bishop's attention that your nephew is not exactly, devout, shall we say? Oh, he tithes his share and he speaks a good game to those who matter, I'll give him that. But t'would not be hard to make a case for heresy; and you know our position on heretics. Purging is the only remedy. Of course," the monk looked sideways at his prey, "the Bishop would expect some measure of gratitude for giving you back Quesnay."

"I don't suppose a thank you note would suffice. What do you want?"

"Oh, nothing really, just some harmless information. For instance, what might you know of your future niece's family? I believe they hold Sedgemoor, just south of here?"

"The MacLure's are a thieving bunch of Scottish trash, that's what I know of them!" Reginald spit into the fire.

"According to our records, they are well liked by their neighbors and give faithfully of their stores to the church."

"There is nothing faithful about the lot of them! Ask them why they left Skye to live in Britain? I doubt they'd admit the truth of it. They ran away and changed their name to escape the judgment due them. Legend says a fortune disappeared with them. I wouldn't put it past them!

"But Sedgemoor was built nearly a hundred years ago by a MacLure. How came you by this folly?"

"I have friends. Besides, I make it my business to know my enemy and Tormond MacLure is chief amongst them," Reginald ground out through his yellowed teeth.

"Traitors to their Clan? Surely, not. They operate well within Church decrees. Those at Avignon seem most happy with them.

"'Tis a wicked farce. I'd swear to it," Reginald whispered, "I hear the girl has some sort of power."

"You speak of witchcraft at Sedgemoor?" the monk smirked.

"They should burn," Reginald suggested happily.

"Indeed, but what proof is there?"

"Do you really need proof? If you give me back Quesnay, I'll deliver the MacLures. Burn Sedgemoor to the ground for all I care," Reginald giggled as his eyes flashed green in the firelight. He caught site of a silver flask within the folds of the monk's robe. He licked his quivering lips in anticipation.

"Oh, where are my manners? Would you like a dram?" He handed over the flask.

"Keep it," he said as he watched Reginald slobber all over it, "And keep our dealings just between us, Baron. Erlick need not know of our conversation."

"Whatever you say," Reginald belched between gulps of amber liquid. "How will I find you when I have what you want?"

"I will find you, Baron." With that, Lucian Medeiro faded into the darkness.

❦   ❦   ❦

"Let's get you settled in," Ruffian smiled, "I know it's been days since you've slept in a decent bed." He led her to a room across the hall from his. She looked at him and grinned. Her eyes were feverishly bright and her cheeks were pink, as if she were blushing. They walked into a round room decorated in shades of deepest plum. Rich linens graced the bed, and the tapestries would rival any of Jolie's handiwork. A small fire had been kindled in the hearth and the gentle scent of beeswax and candlelight filled the air.

"Are you tired? Would you like to rest a bit before dinner?" he asked.

"This room is beautiful, like the color of storm clouds at midnight," she marveled.

"Tessa?"

"Aye, I do think I'll lie down for just a moment. My head will stop aching if I can just sleep on something that's not moving." She climbed upon the high featherbed and sunk into it's warmth. Ruffian perched himself protectively beside her.

"You're not going to watch me sleep."

"Why not?"

"Because it's odd, that's why not."

"You forget, I'm the Baron."

"Uh-huh," she yawned.

"I can do as I please in my own keep."

"Yes you can," she nodded and quickly fell asleep. He gently stroked her hair as he watched her. Her brow seemed to grow hotter as an hour passed, then two.

"Tessa, wake up." He shook her as he called her name again. There was no response. Her breathing was shallow and faint. The fever had grown worse. In moments, Ruffian was down the hall, beating on his mother's door.

"Ruffian, what is wrong?" Jolie asked as she adjusted her shawl.

"It's Tessa, she can't wake up." He was speaking so quickly, his parents had trouble following him.

"What do you mean, she *can't* wake up, son?" Rod asked.

"She can't wake up!" *perhaps yelling it would make them understand,* "She told me she didn't feel well when she arrived. I thought she was just tired from traveling. I thought a nap would do her good, but now I can't seem to rouse her and the fever is getting worse."

"Rod, get the tapestry bag from our room. Ruffian, I need cool water for the basin and some clean cloths. Oh and son, go get Elspeth and Tormond." The men ran off in opposite directions as Jolie laid her hand upon Tessa's brow.

"What did you get yourself into, girl?" she whispered. Jolie closed her eyes and breathed a prayer for guidance and healing, then she began mentally ticking off the stops they'd made along the way. What food had they eaten? *Everyone else is fine*, she thought, *so why is Tessa so sick?*

The MacLures burst into the chamber with Rod and Ruffian close behind. Elspeth too her daughter's hand and peered intently at her.

"Do you know if she ate anything funny on the trip?" Jolie asked as she prepared a poultice of smelly herbs.

"Nay, she ate the same things I did," Elspeth muttered. Jolie noticed an odd look on Elspeth's face and realized she was trying very hard to concentrate on something.

"Would you excuse us for a moment, please?" Jolie asked the men as she shooed them from the room, "We need to examine her more closely."

"Oh," Tormond said as understanding dawned on him, "We'll be right outside."

After shutting the door behind them, Jolie approached the bed. She watched Elspeth. *Could it be she has the gift?* She wondered. She sat down on the edge of the bed and took Elspeth's hand. Elspeth seemed startled by the gesture, but did not let go. Jolie took Tessa's limp hand and the three women formed a circle wrought of blood and faith.

"Lord Almighty, show us how to help Tessa," Jolie asked out loud in the silent room. Fleeting images flowed over both women as they prayed on; the trip, their meals, preparations to leave Sedgemoor, and one unfamiliar scene. A chill breeze grazed their cheeks as they saw Tessa handing out baked confections to the village children.

"What village?" Elspeth whispered to herself.

"It's Selengs. Look, see the weaving circle there by the trees? I'd know it anywhere," Jolie breathed. They watched as the scenes of Tessa and the children flitted in and out of their minds. 'Lord, please show us what You would have us know," Jolie asked. The sky drew darker as they watched a child give Tessa a dipper of water from the stream that meandered nearby. She drank deeply from the dipper and smiled her thanks. The scene faded away and left them alone in the chamber with Tessa still unconscious, by their side.

"Something in the water?" Elspeth looked to Jolie.

"It was contaminated," Jolie nodded, "I wish I knew what was in it. The most we can do is keep her cool and get her to drink. I'll go prepare a meadowsweet infusion to bring her fever down." She headed for the door when Elspeth reached out and stopped her.

"Jolie, what just happened here?"

"I believe, m'lady, that we were just gifted with a vision," she smiled.

"Does that sort of thing happen to you often?"

"Nay, not often," she hesitated to say more, "I'll go get that infusion now."

"Jolie, thank you."

"I didn't do anything but ask for guidance. I believe it was you who said that the Lord alone brings healing." The weaver left the room as Ruffian raced back to Tessa's bedside.

The next few hours were spent spoon-feeding Tessa the infusion of herbs. It was when she started batting the spoon away, that he knew she was improving. Her fever finally broke and she fell into a peaceful sleep. Ruffian succumbed to exhaustion near midnight, while Jolie and Elspeth sat near the hearth and watched their children sleep.

As night passed on, in its ageless dance across the heavens, the shadow of a tall, lean man could be seen tending to the cries of dying children in the village of Selenge. The fever burned brightly there. Artemis worked frantically against the icy hand that attempted to end their existence.

"Rest, friend." Robert all but commanded. The Messenger guided Artemis to the make-shift table in the village square. The opal in his ring flashed with a rainbow of imprisoned fire.

"You know I cannot rest," Artemis muttered.

"Even the mighty *Artemesia* cannot save them all. Selenge is in God's hands. We are but human," Robert reasoned.

"If those who court evil can take a life, is it so insane to think we can save one?"

"One life, yes. But we already know that several have been lost. The bodies were found floating in the stream this morning. Who knows how long they've been dead. I'm not sure, but it's probable that they floated downstream from Thierry. 'Tis why the water made so many sick here."

"What killed those in the stream?" Artemis asked, as he dragged a weary hand through the tangle of silver hair that had long since come down from the neat plates he usually wore. There was silence. Robert sat at the table, but looked off into the distance.

"How did they die, Robert?"

"Some had been impaled by the lance, others burnt or disemboweled. We found one headless."

"My God, who would do this wickedness?"

"They all bear one similarity. We found the mark of judgment on each body. They'd been labeled heretics before their executions."

"Nay! Those living to the north were God-fearing!" he cried.

"You know as well as I do, brother, that faith has naught to do with the holy politics of this land. Sovereign and Papacy will battle on, and we will be blown hither and yon by their whims." Robert hated to be so blunt, but someone had to make Artemis see reality.

"We are but pawns in the game," Artemis sighed, "'Tis a game of life and death they play. I fear it's time for the 33 to make their presence known."

"In due time, my friend."

CHAPTER 13

❀

TREASURES

It took Tessa nearly a week to recover from the fever that had stolen her strength. Her mother had driven her crazy with incessant coddling. When Elspeth was elsewhere; Jolie was lurking nearby.

"All the gold at Sedgemoor for five minutes to myself," she muttered as she watched her mother peer around the corner in her direction.

"Mother, would you send Ethan to my chamber, please?

"Ethan? In your chamber?" Elspeth shot Tessa one of those looks that could curdle milk.

"Oh posh, Mother, and would you be believing I have designs on Ruffian's brother?"

"You must learn not to give even the appearance of evil."

"Speaking to Ethan is evil?" Tessa smirked.

"You may speak with him in the great hall, or not at all."

"*I am an adult, and as such, I will do as I please, when I please!*" If only she could say those words out loud.

The midday meal provided Tessa the good fortune she sought. Ethan was assigned the seat next to her, as if by design. Ruffian had engaged Tormond in a lively debate over the state of the feudal system versus the theory of freewill and self-sufficiency among the working class. Serrah sat re-arranging her cooked cabbage and grouse on Tessa's other side.

"Would you do me a great favor, Ethan?" she whispered as she reached for a pinch of salt.

"Now, m'lady, it would crush my brother if I were to steal you away, though indeed I do understand your feelings." He grinned as she rolled her eyes and made some sort of gagging gesture that only he could see.

"What wouldst thee have me do?" He batted his blue eyes dreamily.

"I will arrange a meeting with any woman you choose if you would but distract this flock of hens from my heels for one brief afternoon. Know you at Sedgemoor, I had my freedom. I came and went as I pleased. I cannot stomach this constant surveillance one moment longer." Ethan knew the girl needed a break.

"*Any* woman I choose?" he confirmed.

"Aye, except me."

"You wound me, lass," he grinned.

"You'll recover, I'm sure."

"This afternoon?"

"Aye, if you think you can manage a bit of theatrics?"

"Hmmm, maybe a spill off my horse or a tumble down the staircase?"

"Let's not go overboard, you don't want the wenches thinking you are an oaf," she smiled.

"What's an oaf?" Serrah leaned over Tessa's shoulder.

"Serrah! It is so rude to eavesdrop. For your information, an oaf is a wise and wonderfully handsome man," Ethan explained. Tessa snorted under her kerchief.

"Oh. Well then, I think you are very much an oaf!" Serrah smiled at her brother.

"I agree with Serrah."

"Do you want my help or not?" he warned.

"I don't care how you do it, but please draw the guards off me for the afternoon. I will owe you for this."

"Oh yes, my sister-to-be, you will indeed."

Just as the ladies were retiring to the solarium for an afternoon of needlework, Ethan cried out in apparent pain. The family swarmed around him as Tessa slipped from the hall. Sounds of muffled voices faded as she made her way farther and farther into the East wing of seldom-used chambers. The third floor was dark and covered with dust and cobwebs. Tessa opened each door and peered inside. Drapes that had been pulled decades before, afforded her little light. Most of the rooms she found were sleeping chambers that she wasn't much interested in. At the end of the damp and chilly hall was a large Oak door. She could no longer hear any sign of life from the rest of the castle below. *So why do I feel the need to tiptoe?* She shook her head. She was on her own in the first time in weeks. The familiar sense of excitement filled her once more. Letting out a less-than-ladylike grunt, she pushed the immense door open and entered another place and time.

Slivers of daylight sliced through the partially shrouded windows. Huge oil paintings sat stacked on one another in the far corner. A large man, dressed as a warrior, regarded her from the first painting. The Quesnay banner waved in the background of the piece. *Adrian La Quesnay?* She wondered as she traced the line of his jaw that was so much like Ruffian's. Another portrait boasted a regal couple seated in large ornate chairs. Frozen in time, the couple peered at Tessa curiously. Some of the paintings were of dogs and hunting scenes. Tessa passed by all the purely decorative pieces until she came to the last framed piece far in the dusty corner.

The framework was a beautiful carved knotwork chain that surrounded the portrait of a very young woman. The canvas had been slashed with a blade repeatedly. *If the owner hated it so much, why keep it at all?* Tessa asked out loud, *Why not burn it and commission a new one?* The girl's face was hauntingly familiar to her. A subtle smile played upon her lips. There was a twinkle of mischief in her eyes, as if she were posing for her lover. The gold of her hair cast a graceful halo around her as the afternoon sun filled the place she had once stood. Dressed in an amazing gown of ice blue, she shimmered in the light. Jewels dripped from the hem and neckline. A silver chain encircled her tiny abdomen and followed the dropped waistline to the ground. Upon her neck lay a silver chain boasting a gryphon's claw. Tessa gasped and stepped back. Her hand flew to her own throat and she touched the chain. *The hair and the eyes. Of course, 'twas Journey on her wedding day. But who would slash her portrait?* She shivered, as a cool draft seemed to caress her shoulders.

"Mayhap Adrian did it in his fit of rage the night he died, or was it Reginald? Did he make his brother watch as he sliced her face to ribbons as a form of twisted torture?" Tessa continued to mutter to herself as she tried to think of a way to restore the portrait. The room turned out to be a treasure trove of the family's belongings from long ago. She found tapestries, furniture and even the matching chairs that Ruffian's grandparent's had sat upon for their portrait. *All these shall be moved back to the great hall,* she decided. A flash of light caught Tessa's eye just as she moved to leave the chamber. She looked again, nearer to the window and saw a beaded tapestry draped over an old chest. Tiny beads of amethyst and quartz dotted the tapestry that was a landscape scene of the seaside cliffs. *It puts my mother's work to shame,* she thought. She moved the heavy fabric aside and opened the dull green sea chest. Among the trinkets and linens from a lifetime of travels, something wrapped in fine sheeting lay in the bottom. Tessa looked behind her, sure that she was being watched. Seeing no one, she lifted the form from the chest. A heavy gown of ice blue spilled into her hands like liquid. Each jewel still in its place from the portrait. Tessa held it up to herself. *Dare I?*

She gathered the gown and Journey's slashed portrait and left the lonely chamber. Slipping down the quiet hallway, she noticed the sun was rather low in the sky; its pink hue cast a glow upon the old stone walls, warming them at least in appearance. Passing dangerously close to the great hall, she heard the staff preparing for the evening meal. *How long have I been gone?* she wondered as she closed her chamber door behind her. No fire was in her hearth and the room was dark. *That's odd, it's not like the staff to forget to warm my room.* She tucked her acquisitions safely behind her gowns in the rosewood armoire.

"Have fun today?" a voice pierced the darkness. Ruffian lit a tallow candle upon the mantle the bent down on one knee to kindle the fire in the cold hearth.

"You nearly scared me to death!" she yelped.

"Now you know how I felt when I couldn't find you all afternoon."

"You didn't involve my parents, did you?"

"Nay, you're safe. Ethan covered for you through his cries of agony," he smirked.

"What?"

"You'll see. I must say that the level of loyalty you inspire in others impresses me. You should think on commanding troops for the Crown; 'Joan of Arc' and all that!" Ruffian closed the gap between them in a few short strides. Tessa actually feared him as her approached her. *The muscle in his jaw is clenching, that cannot be good,* she cringed. He pulled her roughly to him and closed his eyes.

"Never do that to me again," he ground out against her ear. His fingers dug into her arms until she cried out. She could feel his anger in his touch.

"I'm sorry. I just needed some time…"

"You seek time away from me?"

"Nay, Ruffian, just solace. I needed time to think and to plan."

"Plan what, an escape? Having second thoughts, are we?" He looked hurt and angry.

"I was, in truth, planning a bit of our future," she whispered.

"Ah Tessa," he snorted, "Some things you are better off leaving to chance."

"Are you saying you no longer wish to be with me?" She stepped away, not wanting to see his face as he answered.

"What? Did you sniff too much dust in the east wing? Filth must make you daft. I'll make a mental note; no spring cleaning when you are Mistress of La Quesnay. Yes, I knew where you were," he answered her shocked and guilty expression. "Ethan filled me in on your escapade after I nearly destroyed his sleeping quarters looking for you."

"I'm sorry I didn't confide in you. Ethan seemed like the logical choice at the time."

"You asked me if I no longer wanted to be with you. Let me make it clear to you." He took her hand and seated her before the crackling fire.

"You and I will be together. I don't have to plan it all out because its already been planned by someone wiser than you and I."

"Your mother?" she laughed as she wiped her eyes on her sleeve.

"Well, she would say our destiny is to be together. You shall not escape me, lass. Your future is linked to mine. I, for one, refuse to walk away from that truth."

"She would say that it had been foretold; that we were divinely appointed to one another," Tessa smiled.

"Ah yes, and I have learned to agree with mother as much as is humanly possible." He entwined his fingers into her hair and pulled her to his kiss. "I pledge myself to you, Tessa, forever." He was deadly serious now as he promised himself to her. She leaned into him as she deepened the kiss to seal their hearts together. It was a magical moment until her stomach let out a loud and demanding growl.

"Umm…hungry?" he grinned.

"Famished, actually," she blushed.

"Well, then let's join the others for dinner. I'm sure you and Ethan have much to discuss."

"Really?"

"Oh my, yes," he laughed outright as they left the crackling fire behind.

"And may Thee bless us, each one according to Thy will. In Thy name, Amen" Rod finished the grace amid the flickering candlelight of the great hall. Tessa had not had a chance to speak to Ethan before the prayer, but now as they were served their meal, she noticed a servant girl place a large steaming bowl of gruel in front of Ethan. Tessa frowned, *breakfast for dinner?* He looked at her and sighed heavily before returning his attention to his gruel.

"Why are you eating that?" she whispered as the other chatted about the day.

"Poor judgment on my part, I'm afraid," Ethan mumbled into his wooden bowl of goo.

"Have some of the venison, its wonderful with turnips and cheese," she offered.

"Can't eat that for awhile, lass."

"Why not?" She noticed Ruffian watching them from across the long table with a smile.

"What is going on, Ethan?"

"Well, you asked me to create a diversion this afternoon, remember?"

"Yes, but why are you eating gruel? Are your parents punishing you for letting me slip away for a few hours alone?"

"Nay, mother babied me all afternoon after the surgery."

"Surgery?"

"Well, you see, I couldn't think of anything to draw their attention from you. You didn't give me much time to prepare, you know. Anyway, time was running out. The midday meal was ending and so I did the only thing I could think of. I faked a terrible toothache. I said I had cracked a tooth on a chicken bone."

"A toothache. That seems plausible, but where did the surgery come into it? Surely your mother, the healer, wouldn't do more than give you an herbal infusion."

"Well, mother dear might be the healer at Sedgemoor, but out of respect for the people of Quesnay, she deferred to Agnes Groate, the healer here at the keep."

"Oh."

"We managed to talk Agnes out of the leeches, but I didn't make it out of her chamber without treatment. I have a souvenir for you. So you'll never forget my sacrificial service to thee, m'lady." Reaching into the leather pouch on his belt, Ethan placed a molar into Tessa's hand, beneath the table. Ruffian watched the secret exchange. He watched as her eyes widened as she felt the token in her hand. *Priceless*, he grinned as he sipped his ale.

"Oh Ethan, I am so sorry I got you into to this." He saw faint tears starting to form in her eyes. *Never let a good opportunity pass you by, Ethan my boy*, he grinned.

"Anything for you, lass," he said gently. He knew that one day he would collect on this debt, with interest.

Time ambled on as they all worked to restore the keep and the people of Quesnay castle. Ruffian spent most of his days on the training field. Ground combat as well as horseback techniques were strongly addressed. Every male, over the age of eight summers, was armed with sword or longbow. They were taught to handle a dagger as well. Tactical maneuvers were studied and Ruffian paid certain attention to his men's diet and exercise. He could tell by their hair and teeth, that most subsided on the rotting scraps from Reginald's table. Ruffian swore that every family at Quesnay would be well provided for from that time on.

Families were taught in the ways of the church, but it was in everyday occurrences that those from Sedgemoor showed them God's mercy and grace. They began to look for His face in the clouds; His hand upon their lives. Children were being taught their letters and how to cipher. For many, it was the first time they'd ever read or written their own names. The people were valued. As they were supported, so they supported their Laird. God was blessing them beyond all they could ask or imagine.

The great hall was silent as night fell. Before the massive hearth, Tessa and Ruffian sat contentedly watching the flames dance. Everyone, save for the night guard, was asleep for the night. A light snow had just begun to float down upon the land. What peace it bestowed. It was in this silence that the two found some precious time alone.

"My parents shall be wanting to return to Sedgemoor soon, Ruffian. Word has come that my sister in law is with child and shall deliver close to the New Year. Your keep seems to be in fine order now, and there's been no further threat from your Uncle."

"You are correct. My watchers have not seen Reginald since he was banished."

"You know my father will not leave me here alone with you."

"Your father likes me."

"Not that much, I'm afraid," she smiled, "Decisions need to be made soon, or I'll have to return to Sedgemoor. I don't wish to push you, but I want you to be aware of their plans." She watched him as he stepped to the mantle and looked intently into the fire. He raked his hand through his hair as he struggled to form his reply. He then knelt before her in the firelight. Taking her hands; he wanted the moment to be perfect.

"Do you truly think you need to push me to the altar? This has all been for naught, if not for you, Tessa. Quesnay castle means less than nothing without you here. You, my sweet enchantress, with all your intuitions and secret gifts, doth vex me at times! You drive me daft with the scent of your hair. Your eyes reflect your heart and I swear I can see eternity in them. Do me the honor of marrying me. Grant me this wish, Contessa." He watched as the tears began to stream through her smile. He followed a lone teardrop as it trickled down her neck and disappeared to places he'd only dreamt of. He slowly took her face within his strong hands. *How can anyone love someone so completely?* He searched her eyes deeply before capturing her mouth in the deepest of kisses. In a final surrender, she opened her lips as their tongues danced and swirled together. His arms encircled her as his hands slowly moved to the small of her back. He gently pressed her to him.

"Ahem." Tormond stood not ten feet away with a tankard of warm goat's milk and a slice of cook's rum cake in hand.

"A pleasant evening, is it not, children?" he asked as nonchalantly as possible. "I say, daughter, you two look like you have something to celebrate, perhaps?" Setting her away from himself, Ruffian wiped his mouth casually; having at least the good grace to look embarrassed and said,

"M'lord, we've had this conversation before. You know full well what my intentions have been and still are regarding Tessa. As you can see, I think I can protect and provide for her as you would wish."

"Aye, son, I believe you want the best for her as I do."

"Then, with your permission, we wish to marry."

"And what say you, daughter? Does this rouge and scoundrel fit the bill?" Tormond grinned, knowing the answer all too well.

"Father, there has never been another."

"Then a wedding there shall be," Tormond commanded. She jumped into her father's arms, nearly knocking his cake and milk to the floor.

"Easy, child! You don't dare waste perfectly good rum cake!"

Though Jolie was as happy about the joining as Elspeth was, something dampened her spirit. Her sleep was interrupted with dreams of Atremis in battle. She'd never known a more peace-loving man in her life, yet here she saw him fighting to the death with some unseen enemy. The shadowy form never came into focus in the dreams, yet she felt the cold chill of death around her friend. It had been several weeks since she received word from him. His last missive had been cryptic and flat, without his usual flare. He told her about the sickness at Selenge and the massacre to the north at Thierry. It confirmed the vision they'd had in Tessa's room. Then, that very morning, a runner came with word from him. A parchment tied with wool twine was delivered to Jolie's hand. A sick feeling welled up in the pit of her stomach.

My dearest friend Jolie,

Selenge stands silent against the cold sky as I make ready to leave this place for good. Only the strongest survived the poison that flowed from the hate at Thierry village. We convinced them to go to Sedgemoor for safety. Most of the children are gone. I cannot erase their cries. I've begun to question my purpose in the grand scheme of things. I made little difference in Selenge. I was powerless to help them. My whole life, I've stood back from the fray. I've analyzed men's motives and fooled myself into thinking I was above it all. My home is full of journals recording the history of the 33. But have I once joined my brothers to fight against the evil that kills? Nay.

I'm not questioning my faith. Rest assured the only thing I question is my role; my mission in regard to that faith. Sometimes you must stand up and take action. I see no other way to reconcile the travesty at Selenge and Thierry. You may not see me for awhile, friend, but take heart that I am following the path laid out for me. I know no other way to live. I will contact you when and if I can. Until then, be strong in spirit and mention me in your prayers. Check on the observatory if you would, I hear tell of a blazing star that should pass overhead near the Yuletide.

As ever I remain,

A.

Jolie slowly rolled the yellow parchment into a narrow tube. She secured it with the wool twine that reminded her of Atremis' shoes. She smiled faintly and shook her head.

"Godspeed, my friend," she whispered.

Ruffian felt confident that the men of Quesnay could now hold off a siege if the need arose. The MacLures and Bardougnes made ready to return to Sedgemoor for the wedding. Tessa looked around the castle that would soon be her home. New tapestries hung next to ancient ones in the great hall. She left Journey's ruined portrait with a local painter and he promised he could restore it. She commanded that all the La Quesnay belongings be brought back to the great hall from storage, before their return. *It shall be a proper Baronial Manor, once again,* she assured herself. In a short time, she would become its Mistress, the Lady of La Quesnay Manor.

CHAPTER 14

❀

PROVIDENCE

Decembre 1309
Wilderness of Dundrennan

The once brightly painted wagons had seen their better days. The women were thrown violently as the wagon leading the small caravan slid into yet another rut in the road. God had been merciful and held back the mind-numbing snows of early winter. They'd only seen sparse flurries, but the chill was ever present. Belinda Stolford began to reconsider the prudence of slipping away from court at harvest time. The weather only reflected her heart, as she realized she had successfully run away from home, and no one bothered to look for her. The weeks since then had been hard, but rewarding, as Belinda began a journey to herself. She remembered thinking it providence that the travelers had happened by, just when they did. They had taken her into their fold without question. The cast-offs from society had been her salvation. A group of roughly 15 people, the travelers were composed of all manner of humanity. Some were well educated, which would slip out when they'd speak. Other's hands were far too smooth to be considered common folk. There were accents from afar, mixed with the slang of the local working class. They traveled by navigation of the stars, believing they were on some sort of mystic pilgrimage. Belinda learned how to survive by using her wits and her other obvious charms, as Dalibar Toman, the group's leader, put it. Belinda opted not to use her body, but her voice instead. Singing was just one more talent she'd never been allowed to discover at Court.

"Why so quiet, Belinda?" Kryston asked. Kryston Eichel had been a nun sent to minister at the village of Bogdon, but by the time she arrived there, only a handful of its inhabitants were alive. Cloaked warriors had destroyed the village only hours before. The men swore revenge and disappeared into the woods to pursue their attackers. Kryston gathered the females and began the trek back to the abbey. Along the way, she found homes for most of the girls. People were always looking for servants to tend their homes and chores. By the time she'd reached the outskirts of London, only Brynn was with her. The Abbot was not impressed with Kryston's tale of woe. In fact, he called her a failure and slammed the abbey door in her face. He said they were lucky leave with their hides intact, for squandering church funds for naught. The girls walked aimlessly for what seemed like hours before being approached by Dalibar and his family. Without hesitation, the group took them in and fed them. Half a year had passed since that night and the two had been with them ever since.

"Hmm? Oh! Sorry, just remembering how things used to be, that's all," Belinda sighed.

"Do you miss it?" Kryston loved to hear tales from court.

"Not terribly, no, but sometimes even the awful is somehow comforting, if it's all you are used to. I really have no right to complain. I was never actually mistreated, just totally ignored. They probably haven't even noticed I'm gone yet," she smiled bitterly.

"You know you can stay with us as long as you like. I doubt I shall ever leave the family now, and I think dear Brynn may be interested in Stefan," she whispered.

"She's so young."

"I should think that by now you've learned that life is short. Stefan is a kind man. The Rom hold family above all else," Kryston answered, "She'll be a good wife and have many babies. The world is changing, Belinda, you must change too. You must change your attitudes, for instance, what do you think of Michelassi, our new troubadour? His voice is so full and rich, you two would blend well, I'd wager, in more ways than one."

"I'm not interested."

"I believe your chances of marrying nobility flew out the window when you did, last fall."

"I'm still not looking for a husband, be he noble or farmer."

"He watches you, you know. When you sing; when we dance around the fire at night, his eyes are always on you," Kryston informed her.

"Something's wrong with that man."

"What? He's beautiful! Dark and handsome, he could have his pick of women."

"I think it's his eyes. Even when he smiles, his eyes are cold," Belinda said.

"I think you're searching for any excuse to remain lonely."

"You don't know how very wrong you are." She got up and made her way over to where Tamera was sewing. Belinda had traded her belongings one by one to merchants for things the group needed like food, tools, horses and material for more clothing. Tamera was finishing up a new skirt for Belinda, as a way of thanks. She'd never had clothes so vivid before. The top was a loosely woven lavender peasant blouse that draped provocatively off Belinda's creamy shoulders. The Skirt was full and ruffled; the deep indigo blue was accented by lavender trim. When she'd tried them on, she felt like a different person.

"Almost done!" Tamera smiled.

"It's beautiful, but I'm not sure I'm brave enough to wear it."

"When the time is right, you shall wear it," she smiled and winked wickedly.

"Travelers on the road!" Dalibar called back to Zavier and Stefan.

Ruffian raised his hand to halt the group traveling to Sedgemoor for the wedding.

"Trouble?" Ethan asked.

"We shall see, little brother." Ruffian rode on ahead to meet the group that were trying to free their wagon from the wet, muddy rut in the road.

"Need some help, friend?" he asked as got closer.

"Thank you, no. My men almost have it free. I am Dalibar Toman and this is my family."

"Rapheal LaQuesnay," Ruffian nodded, "I see we are headed in the same direction. Where are you going?"

"We go where the wind takes us, sir, and you?" Dalibar smiled. His coal black hair was pulled back from his face with a leather thong, but gentle waves had worked their way free and framed his dark face. His soulful eyes looked to Ruffian and searched him for signs of a confrontation. Dalibar could be the fiercest of enemies if called upon. *His teeth are amazingly white, for a gypsy,* Ruffian thought.

"We hail from Sedgemoor." Ruffian opted not to share more information than was necessary to be polite. Highwaymen of some sort were always accosting travelers. The men freed the wagon and they pulled a few feet ahead. Dalibar saluted Ruffian with a flick of his ringed hand and boarded the waiting wagon.

"Go in peace, my friend," he called back to Ruffian.

"It's getting late and the women are hungry," Ethan called.

"The *women* are hungry?" Ruffian smirked.

"Okay, so I'm hungry, is that a crime?" Ethan caught site of a girl in the last wagon. She looked so familiar but he couldn't place her face. "Why don't we ask them to share our fire for the night?"

"Why on earth would we do that?" Ruffian looked at his brother.

"Why wouldn't we?"

"They're gypsies."

"And?"

"And we have the Laird of Sedgemoor and his family under our protection. I say we do not invite trouble."

"Stolford!" Ethan yelped.

"What?"

"The girl in that wagon, I'd swear she's Zerlinda Stolford!"

"Ah, that's *Belinda* Stolford, you dolt, and it couldn't be her," Ruffian rolled his eyes.

"I'll wager the silver in my pouch that it is."

"Only one way to find out." Ruffian rode ahead to the caravan and approached Dalibar's wagon. Belinda ducked her head quickly as he rode past. She wanted to melt right into the creaking floorboards of the wagon. *I'll be back at court before the first snow flies if they realize who I am,* Belinda cringed and snuggled deeper into her black woolen cloak. Ruffian passed her without acknowledgment and approached Dalibar.

"Would you care to share a camp this evening, friend? We have plenty of food and I can hear music from one of your wagons. We'd love to hear some lively tunes under the moonlight." Dalibar, never being one to turn down a free meal agreed immediately. "There's a grove of oak trees just after the road curves ahead. Stop there and we will join you for the evening," Ruffian directed as he turned and rode back to Ethan and the others.

"Why are we stopping?" Rod asked Ruffian.

"Because it's getting late and the women are hungry."

"And we're making camp with them?"

"Yes, father, we are."

"Why would we do that?"

"Why not?"

"They're gypsies," Rod assumed this was a logical answer.

"They are people, father, just like us; a family traveling on the road. Aren't you the one who taught us to be tolerant of others? And there is safety in numbers."

"You're right, of course, son." He looked at Ethan and Ruffian who had assumed the faces of choirboys. "Something's going on, but if you're sure we are safe, then I'll let you have your fun," Rod confided, then pulled the wagon ahead of his sons who were on horseback.

"Very diplomatic," Ethan laughed.

The two groups fashioned a campsite in the oak grove, just off the road. Ruffian knew the spot well, and directed the men to a cache of firewood just over the rise. They were approaching Sedgemoor land now, and he knew its borders like nothing else. He knew he had the upper hand, should any trouble arise with the strangers. Ruffian smiled mildly as he scanned the horizon. *If it is Belinda with them, honor compels me to seek her safe release,* he decided, *besides, I have a wager to win.*

Belinda tried her best to stay hidden in the shadow of the wagons, but anonymity was not meant to be.

"Mistress Stolford?" Elspeth touched Belinda's sleeve. She turned before thinking but could not meet Elspeth's concerned eyes.

"Aye, m'lady," she whispered.

"By the Saints, what are you doing with these people?" she hissed, "If you've been taken against your will, rest assured the men will secure your freedom. You can accompany us back to our home and Tormond will send word to your parents."

"Nay, m'lady, I'm here because I wish to be. I left court last autumn."

"With your parents approval?" Elspeth cocked a well-shaped eyebrow, in that way only mothers do.

"I am eighteen summers old."

"Aye, and?"

"And nay, the truth be told, my parents are unaware of my recent decision to ah, *travel*."

"I see. So what, pray thee, would you have us do?" Elspeth asked.

"I'm begging you, m'lady, to let this be. I did what I had to do."

"Were you mistreated at court? Did a man…?"

"Nay! No man has ever touched me in that way," she sounded almost sad over that fact.

"I cannot explain it, only to say that one night something welled up inside of me, and I knew I had to escape the entrapment set before me if I was ever to live a life of integrity."

"And you choose to become a Gypsy?" Elspeth questioned.

"'Tis the only time in my life that I have been accepted, nay, loved, for exactly who and what I truly am." Tears threatened in Belinda's eyes, but she lifted her chin and stood there, waiting for Elspeth's decision. The MacLure's had the power to return her to either her parents or back to court. Her brief taste of freedom could have end that very night. It was more words than Elspeth had heard Belinda utter in all the years she'd known her. Ever content to stay in her sister, Hester's shadow, Belinda was most often seen and not heard. *Something has changed her*, Elspeth thought as she weighed the options.

"I will speak to Laird MacLure on your behalf. Believe me when I say we do not wish cause you distress. I'm not sure traveling with a band of gypsies is the safest place to be, but I respect your desire for freedom. I will come to you by morning with word." Elspeth could not suppress the urge to hug the trembling girl. She knew, full well the role young ladies were expected to play at court. Her own guardians had secured her a place there, more to be rid of her than any other reason. Many a girl acquired a suitable husband through those means. Most often though, they were marriages in name only. They were in truth, business deals, created to benefit both families with wealth, power or political protection in one form or another.

Elspeth had proven a bit too outspoken for court, however, but before being turned out into the street, she had caught the eye of a certain returning commander for the Crown. Tormond had recognized her as one from his own clan. He offered her his protection as she traveled back home. During the days that followed, they'd become fast friends. She felt nothing but safe, traveling with the son of the Laird of Sedgemoor. He was always a gentleman, a Knight in every way, shape and form. She hated for their time together to end. Her guardians were furious that she'd let her mouth ruin her chances for wrangling a husband in London. At 17, they were well ready to be rid of the chit for good. John, her foster father, was so angry he dragged her behind their wattle and daub house to teach her a lesson in humility. Every blow hammered home the lie that she was unlovable, unworthy and would forever be alone. Why, even her own father had abandoned her after her mother had died. She was eight when William had left her with John and his shrew of a wife. She watched as he slowly rode away, never looking back at his only child. It was the last time she ever saw him. No family left, Elspeth was truly alone.

Tormond had thought she would only receive a firm scolding for her cheek, but as he turned to ride away, he heard the cruel words and then the crack of the leather strap against the girl. Immediately he whirled his mount around to the back of the house. Elspeth lay in a crumpled heap on the ground. Blood was seeping through her torn shift. John, in his rage, made the mistake of lashing out at Tormond's horse to drive him away. It was the last mistake he made on MacLure land. John and his wife were escorted out of Sedgemoor within hours. Tormond carried Elspeth to the castle immediately. Her wounds were cleaned and dressed, but it was Tormond's love that finally brought true healing. She would've considered herself lucky to serve the Laird's family. It was beyond her imagining that they would hold her in much higher regard. Tormond had shared the cruel words thrown at Elspeth with his father, Alisdare MacLure. The Laird of Sedgemore called her into his study one night after the evening meal.

"Sit thee down child," Alisdare said as he motioned her nearer the fire, "Let me look at you. Ah, yes, so like your mother, ye are," he shook his head, "such a pity to lose her so young. Your father could not bear life here without her. He had to go, *my dear one*, he was of no earthly good to you as he was. The light had gone out of his eyes the day he buried her. But I want you to be clear on one thing, he did not just abandon you. At the time, John had been a close friend. The years of toil and living with that serpent, Phoebe, drove the man to drink; heavily. I called you here to tell you that you've nothing further to fear from your guardians, as they have surrendered your custody to me. After all, *a Celestine* should be raised as such."

"But my father's surname was Essex." Elspeth looked confused.

"Aye lass, but your mother; she was a Celestine. Someday, *that* will mean something to you."

Belinda and the others prepared a simple mulled wine, as the women from Sedgemore prepared a quick meal for them all to share around the main fire. Dalibar's men did nothing to aid the group ready the campsite, but opted to tune their instruments instead. Ethan watched Belinda's movements with keen interest. His stare unnerved her even more than Elspeth's questions. How she prayed that Tormond would turn a blind eye on the situation and just let her go.

"The meal is ready," Jolie called and clapped her hands to gain their attention.

It is our custom to pray before meals, I trust that will not bother you?" Tormond turned to Dalibar.

"As you wish, sir. Do not change your practices on our account," he smiled. Tormond asked a blessing on the food and safe travels for themselves and their new acquaintances. Jolie caught a glimpse of Kryston crossing herself as the prayer ended.

"What a curious collection of people," Jolie whispered to her husband.

"Indeed," he nodded.

The meal was simple fare of dried, smoked rabbit and roasted onions. Dalibar's men then assembled near the fire for an evening of wine and music. A man named Dougal propped a *bodhran*, or Celtic drum, upon his knee. The stick he used was short and thick, and he used both ends to bring forth an intricate, flowing rhythm. Others played a lute, a recorder, and several fiddles. Tamera carried clochetes; small bells that jingled as she began to dance around the fire. Brynn handed Belinda the tambourine.

"Go on, dance for the people."

"Nay, Brynn, you go. You are much better than I," Belinda tried to sound casual, though a growing hysteria began to rise in her throat. Ethan's eyes were ablaze as the fire reflected in them, but the girl equally caught someone else's attention. Michelassi, the newest troubadour to join their ranks, stared with dark anticipation. She felt like a trapped animal, with nowhere to run.

"Stefan has asked me to walk with him in the moonlight. I'd rather walk than dance," Brynn giggled.

"Be careful, and don't let him…*take anything*." Belinda suddenly sounded older than her 18 years. Brynn nodded solemnly then giggled again as she ran off in Stefan's direction. Belinda gently placed the tambourine upon one of the blankets and started for her wagon. *Would this day never end?* She wondered as she rubbed her aching behind, hoping to ease the bruises from the awful wagon ride on rutted dirt roads.

"May I be of assistance, m'lady?" Ethan asked as he was following her.

"You most certainly may not!" she hissed, "What gall you have, sir, to suggest such a thing."

"So, I was right. You are Mistress Stolford. As a gypsy, you'll appreciate this; I predict I will be coming into some money on the morrow," he smiled.

"I am not a gypsy," she ground out over the din of the distant music.

"Nay? You travel with them, and in case no one has told you, your attire is most assuredly *not* the latest style at court. You seem well adapted to a sojourner's lifestyle. By the way, how was London when last you were there?"

"Oppressive, but thank you for asking," Belinda mumbled as a shadow caught her eye near her wagon. "If you would excuse me, sir, I was just retiring for the evening. It was ever so good to see you and your family once again, but I will be leaving with my friends at dawn. I wish you Godspeed on your journey to Sedgemoor." She moved away from Ethan in time to see a shadowy figure stepping from the wagon she shared with the other women. *I told Brynn to be careful with Stefan. If he's bedded her already…*her thoughts were interrupted as she finally caught sight of the intruder in the moonlit grove of oak.

Michelassi ambled casually back to the music and laughter. He looked back at her and smiled. *It's in his eyes. Even when he smiles, his eyes are cold and dark.* She hugged herself against the chill that came over her. Ethan, not to be so easily dismissed, had watched the exchange. When the wine had run out, and everyone went to bed, Ethan stationed himself as close to the gypsy wagons as propriety would allow. He decided the troubadour would not make another visit to Belinda Stolford that night.

Dawn crept ever so gently over the land of Dundrennan. The pale winter sun managed to lighten the sky to a moderate shade of grey. Clouds heavy with snow seem to loom overhead as the travelers broke camp and made ready to leave.

"You win this time, whelp, but someday this gaming will get you into trouble," Ruffian preached as he tossed his brother a few pieces of silver.

"Amen to that," Tormond agreed as he stood over Ethan, who was stiff and groggy from the night's watch. He managed to scramble from the ground in time to ask Tormond about Belinda's fate.

"Surely we'll be bringing Mistress Stolford to Sedgemore with us until she can be returned to her parents," he offered.

"The girl can think for herself. Elspeth has assured me she is of sound mind. I daresay if Westly and Roxanne Stolford were my parents, I'd slip away as well," Tormond reasoned.

"With all due respect, m'lord, you can't believe she will be better off with them, as with us." Tormond cocked a bushy auburn eyebrow at Ethan, then to his brother.

"What interest do you have in the Stolford situation?"

"None, Sir, no more than knightly concern deems me have," Ethan answered simply.

"Bah!" Ruffian snorted, "I remember you mentioning her after that fiasco last spring!"

"She is lovely," Tormond agreed.

"There is nothing between us!" Ethan blurted out and stormed off.

"Mayhap we should take her with us." Tormond murmured, "She would be free to leave of course, but it might prove to be quite an interesting saga if she were to encounter Ethan in his natural habitat."

All Ruffian could think of was a lifetime of Hester Stolford being his new kin. Tormond and Dalibar discussed the matter in the gypsy's wagon as the others finished packing. Ethan kept busy tending the horses with Rod.

"What is going on?" Tessa asked Ruffian, "Father is speaking to Dalibar. Is he trading horses or something?"

"Ah, *something* like that," Ruffian whispered as he placed a gentle kiss at her temple.

CHAPTER 15

❀

THE FALLEN STAR

They arrived at Sedgemoor just before sunset. Dark clouds of steely grey began to release soft, crystalline flakes. Home had never looked so good to Tormond. He was getting too old to go gallivanting across the countryside, as he had in younger years.

"Time is best spent near hearth and home, my love," he told Elspeth as they entered the bailey.

"Aye, my darling, still…I would rather not *entertain guests* so close to the nuptials." She wasn't sure if her anxiousness stemmed from Tessa's impending marriage, or that Dalibar's entire entourage had followed them home.

"Hush, love. They want nothing more than shelter from the snow and a warm meal. Besides that, it was the only way I could manage getting Belinda here, short of *paying* for her."

"That is ghastly!" Elspeth scoffed.

"Still and all, it would've been my only alternative. Though I would've done it if need be, *even I* feel it would've proven a bit humiliating for the lass to be bought and sold like a prize cow."

"Is Ethan really interested in her? She's a beauty, I'll admit, but surely he remembers the horrible family she hails from."

"Mayhap he wishes to save her."

"Jolie shall pitch a fit!" she laughed.

"And, praytell, why does that fact give you so much pleasure?" he asked.

"I don't know, but it does."

Rod directed the travelers to the stables. The two crofter's cottages stood nearby were kept vacant just for wanderers who the MacLures, by tradition, were required to shelter and feed. As borders and alliances continued to change around them, Tormond decided it was best not to welcome strangers directly into the castle proper. The land was full of tales of friendly gatherings turned to bloody massacres of betrayal. Dalibar seemed harmless enough, but Tormond would take no chances on the eve of his daughter's wedding. The cottages were more than the travelers had been allowed to enjoy in several months time. Everyone was pleased, except for Michelassi, who saw his opportunities to seduce Belinda dwindling away as she was led to the keep.

"Is she not a part of us?" he threw out to Dalibar.

"Silence, you fool. She is the reason we will be warm and fed for as long as I can manage it. Do nothing to anger the Laird, or you shall answer to the family for it, and they can be so *unforgiving*." Dalibar's face turned even darker as he made his meaning clear. Michelassi's eyes turned cold as he stared back at the gypsy.

"As you wish. I'll be sleeping with the horses," he stated flatly and left the cottage.

"Follow him, Stefan, let's see what our friend is up to," Dalibar said, "I'll not have him bring shame upon us here, with these kind people." Stefan waited a few moments, then slipped from the cottage into the darkness. He spotted Michelassi in the stables searching through his pack. At once, the troubadour lifted a heavy-looking pendant into the air and gazed upon it. The torch light flashed upon the silver cross encrusted with rubies. Michelassi hurriedly donned the pendant and slipped it inside the neckline of his russet tunic. Stefan ducked into the shadows as Michelassi left the stables and headed for the stone chapel behind the keep. Many of the tombstones stood shrouded in thick growths of ivy, now brown and withered by winter's hand. Michelassi passed by Journey's rose quartz marker without a second glance. Stefan watched from a distance. The troubadour stepped into the dark chapel and closed the thick, studded door. *He never struck me as a praying man;* Stefan spat on the ground and watched.

The chapel was dark, except for the myriad of small candles near the stone altar. Bryan Delyth was straightening the linens at the altar when he felt the presence of another in the cold and damp room.

"Bless me, Father, for I have sinned," Michelassi recited as he approached Sedgemoor's priest.

"I'm sorry, my son, come back tomorrow…" Bryan said as he turned to see a face from his past. "Can it be?" his eyes widened, "Father Medeiros, what on earth are you doing here?" The man pulled the cross from under his tunic; the rubies caught fire in the candlelight. Bryan immediately knelt before his mentor of days gone by.

"I didn't come here to have my ring kissed, Delyth, get up."

"Has something happened?" Bryan asked, "Am I to be reassigned?"

"Nay. I'm here on another matter for the church. Someone has brought charges against the family you minister to. I am here to find out the truth. I trust I can count on you to be discreet while I'm here?"

"Of course, Father, but what are the charges? I've been with the MacLures since taking my vows and I've found nothing amiss here. The people of Sedgemoor are God-fearing folk," Bryan's voice inched higher as he strove to defend Tormond and the others.

"Aye, but which "God" do they swear allegiance to? There are rumors that the women are soothsayers. It really comes as no surprise, after all the Celts are, and always will be nothing but pagan dogs. I don't see why Edward lets them live. Why the MacLures are really MacLeods who didn't even have the decency to stay in their cursed highlands and defend their own home. I here tell they slipped away from Skye in the night, changed their name to hide their identity, *and* brought a sizable treasure along for the ride as well!"

"That cannot be true. I know these people. Sedgemoor has been here for nigh onto 100 years! Even if that had occurred, the people living here now would have no recollection of such a thing."

"Withholding a true and rightful tithe to the church would be a serious offense. And if the women are conjuring spirits to bring them second sight, it would be our duty to purge the evil from our midst."

"There is no evil among them, I'd swear to it," Bryan insisted. He could feel the hairs stand up on the back of his neck as Michelassi moved closer and looked into his eyes.

"A trusting soul, such as yours can be easily blinded by deceit. Mayhap you've been bewitched?"

"I will prove it to you, then."

"Better that I root out what devils there be. There may still be Druid activity at the castle. You would surely become a target if they thought you were aware of their actions. I am here under another identity, therefore I am safe from their witchery."

"You are wrong about this, Father Medeiro," Bryan promised his teacher.

"The church is never *wrong*, my son, haven't you learned that by now?" Lucian grinned, "Keep my presence here a secret and you can name your price. I cleansed Thierry, and believe me that I will cleanse Sedgemoor as well."

An hour later, the great hall was ready for a dinner to celebrate the upcoming wedding. The bans had been published throughout Sedgemoor and La Quesnay land telling of the impending union. Edward had given his approval after reviewing the proof of Ruffian's true parentage. Even Artemis had heard word of it, as he rode across a foreign wilderness in an effort to find the true purpose of his existence. Tormond invited the travelers in for the meal merely for entertainment, and so as not to appear inhospitable. The fare of roasted quail, bread, hard cheese and ale were quickly thrown together for the larger-than-expected crowd. Tessa was allowed to be seated next to her betrothed. He grazed her knee with the back of his hand as they shared a trencher of quail.

"Not long now, *gra' mo Chroi*, we shall dine like this always," Ruffian purred in her ear. The Gaelic term meaning *love of my heart* warmed her very soul. She watched as Ruffian expertly stabbed the roasted bird with his eating dagger and secured a tasty morsel. She looked down at her place and noticed she was without a utensil for herself. Somewhat bewildered, she looked to Ruffian who had lifted his blade as if to feed her.

"I can feed myself, m'lord."

"Really? I see you have no blade, lass, allow me to assist you," he slowly smiled. He gently lifted the sumptuous bit of quail to her lips. He watched intently as she took it into her mouth.

"Ahem, would you be so kind as to pass the ale?" Ethan smirked, "Oh and, Tessa, would you like to borrow my blade? As you know I will not have a use for it for awhile." His bowl of gruel sat there mocking him.

"She doesn't need your pig-sticker, you clod."

"Alas, my darling, but it appears that I do, unless of course you want to feed me my entire meal. And though I might not object, my Father does not look amused at our little intimacy." Tormond sat glowering from the head of the large table.

"Aye, point well taken. Allow me to gift you with this." Ruffian slipped Journey's dagger into Tessa's hand. "It was my mother's," he whispered.

"I can't accept this…" she began.

"She'd want you to have it."

"But it's all you have of her; it's all that's left of the Jordan family."

"Ah, notice the motto on the blade. *Percussus resurgio; The beaten rise again.* I'm sure the Jordan family yet exists, even as it exists within me," Ruffian explained. "Keep it, if only for protection." Tessa felt like a thief. First she was given Journey's pendant, and now she held the blade of Journey's family. *Will wearing her gown at the wedding be too much?* she wondered. It was if Tessa was stepping into Journey's life, marrying a La Quesnay and moving to the manor. She felt a draft caress her cheek, and a chill went through her.

"Tell me, Toman, would your group honor us with some music this eve?" Tormond asked.

"Of course, sir, it would be our pleasure to entertain you," Dalibar said as he flicked his ringed hand in the air. Immediately his followers assembled to the right of the dais. The area in front of the great hearth served as their stage. Zavier and Stefan joined Kryston and Brynn in a lively Romanian tune. Dalibar spoke quickly to Tamera and then seated himself near Tormond.

"Make haste, Belinda, we need to change for the dance," Tamera whispered as she grabbed Belinda's hand and started for the door.

"I am not dancing here."

"Dalibar says you are."

"I left London because I was tired of being controlled."

"Dalibar said that you either dance, or you part ways with us forever." They were nearly to the door of the cottage when Belinda stopped.

"They will think me lowly and base born."

"Do you think me lowly?" Tamera asked her friend.

"Of course not, I didn't mean…"

"Then you shall dance, and be proud," Tamera threw her the new blouse and skirt she made, "and you will be stunning in this."

The travelers had finished their third number when the women returned to the hall. Ethan had watched Belinda leave but hadn't seen her return. He was on his second tankard of ale when Tamera began a rhythmic beat with the tambourine. The others began a slow and seductive melody with a low undercurrent of the drum. Tamera swayed and danced around an imaginary circle on the floor in front of the hearth. It was the closest they could get to dancing around a fire, as they were used to. Belinda stood behind a large expanse of drapery. She said a prayer and took a deep breath before stepping out to join

Tamera. Those from Sedgemoor gasped when they saw her. Her chestnut hair hung in gentle waves down her back, and swayed as she did, to the seductive music. The dark blue and lavender skirt billowed in spiraling wonder as she turned and weaved around Tamera. The firelight cast a warm glow upon her bare shoulders. Ethan swallowed hard as he watched. Ruffian nudged Tessa and rolled his eyes.

"I do believe he's drooling."

"Is that the same mouse that was here last spring?" Tessa whispered.

"Aye, I think she's *bloomed*. Apparently leaving court was a good decision."

Though frightened at first, as Belinda allowed herself to be enveloped in the music, she relaxed and enjoyed her movements. It was if the strangers at Sedgemoor did not exist, and she was dancing around the campfire with the travelers alone. Her smokey eyes were half closed when she saw Ethan. He looked to be in some sort of hypnotic state as he watched her swaying, but when the music faded away, awe turned to jealousy, and Ethan stalked over to where Belinda and Tamera were.

"Cover thyself, woman," he commanded.

"And who are you, sir, to command anything of me?" Belinda sniffed.

"Belinda, I'm begging you. You don't know what effect you have on…I mean to say that men will look upon you as…" he lowered his voice as he stammered. He ushered her beyond the drapery for a moment of privacy as another round of ale was poured in the great hall.

"You are so beautiful, but also so young. You don't understand what you're doing."

"I am eighteen summers old, sir. I am old enough to be wed and busy with a brood of my own by now. Surely I am old enough to understand the things you speak of."

"What has happened to you?" he asked. Sadness filled his brown eyes.

"You assume too much, m'lord."

"Don't leave with them, Belinda."

"I don't need you to save me, Ethan."

"Mayhap, 'tis I who is in need of saving," he whispered as his lips brushed against hers.

At that moment, Michelassi stepped around the heavy drapery and claimed Belinda's hand. "Dalibar requests we sing."

"I have to go."

"Please think on what we've discussed, Belinda. I'll be waiting." The gypsies struck up a lovely ballad about two lovers separated by untimely death. Michelassi took a certain amount of pleasure in directing the poignant lines at Ethan, as he slowly stroked Belinda's bare shoulder while they sang. She tried to step away from the troubadour, but he simply twirled her gracefully and brought her back to his side. She saw the pain in Ethan's eyes. *It's better this way*, she thought, *mayhap in another time and place, but I cannot stay here.* She snuggled closer to the troubadour as they finished the tune. The hall erupted in applause. She watched Ethan walk out as Tamera gave her an enormous hug. The gathering broke up around midnight. Belinda was staying with Tessa until the wedding. She wearily trudged the winding turret stairs to Tessa's chamber, when a hand shot out of the shadows and covered her mouth. She tried to scream but only managed a muffled squeal. A muscled arm dragged her backward into another passageway. She tried to bite, but couldn't manage to open her mouth wide enough. She lost a leather slipper as she scrambled to free herself. Her assailant retrieved it and slipped it into his cloak. Up more stairs and into darkness the brute dragged her. *Oh my God, it's Michelassi! He's going to rape me, or worse. I didn't mean anything before! 'Twas only to end Ethan's attentions! If he defiles me, he may as well kill me too. What life would I have left if I be soiled this night? God please, where's Ethan when I need him?*

They burst through a heavy door into the starlight. The snow clouds had traveled on, and all was clear and bright. There was not a sound except for the gasps for air as Belinda's abductor released his prize. The cloaked figure blocked the exit and turned to face her.

"Oh, *bloody hell!*" she shrieked.

"Now before you run off, let me explain. Oh and, here is your shoe."

"You bastard."

"The Gypsies taught you to curse like that, didn't they?"

"Let me off this roof at once, or I shall scream," Belinda threatened, as she hopped around on one foot trying to put her slipper back on.

"Oh, they won't come. The guards know I'm here with you."

"Then I shall jump! How will you explain *that* to your Laird?"

"A bit over-dramatic, don't you think?"

"Dalibar will make you pay for this!" she spat.

"Um, actually, I already have paid for the pleasure of your company this evening."

"What?"

"If it's any consolation, you commanded a rather tidy sum," he smiled, "your leader drives a hard bargain for his women." At that, Belinda flew into a rage that scared even her. Never before had such raw anger risen to the point where she was totally out of control. Before Ethan could blink, she was on him like a rabid animal. She ripped off his cloak and it sailed across roof. Her nails tore at his crimson tunic, as every vile accusation she could think of came spewing out. She raked her hand across his beautiful face and left tiny ribbons of blood in her wake.

"I am not one of *his women!*" she hissed, ready to strike again, "I belong to no one."

"Yes, sad isn't it? But that leads me to my next point," he replied, "If you wanted to, you could belong here. You could belong to me. Come and look upon Sedgemoor land." Ethan pushed her toward the battlements. "Can you see the cliffs? Beyond them lies the Tywynn Sea. I hope to sail it one day. And there; can you make out the abbey beyond the castle wall? Here, use this." He pulled out his spyglass and handed it to her. She raised it to hit him with, but his strong hand caught her tiny wrist in midair.

"'Tis not a weapon, it brings images closer as you look through it." He placed the glass to her eye and gently pointed her toward Dundrennan moor. "Can you make out the oak that stands there, on the rise?"

"Where did you get such a thing?" she asked as she scanned the horizon glittering in the moonlight.

"A friend of my mother's gave it to me for my sixteenth birthday. Artemis said he acquired it in Carthage, I think he traded it for a set of knuckle bones, or something"

"Knuckle bones? How revolting!" Belinda looked at him.

"They are used in gaming; likened to dice," he assured her. "Belinda, I brought you here so you could see how beautiful it is. I want you to stay here with me. I'm sure you leaving London severely altered your parent's plans for you. My parents are firm believers in marriage for love or naught at all. We could be together. Tormond would see to it, if we wish it to be." She stopped struggling and looked at him. His brown curls glimmered softly against his collar. He was gorgeous in the moonlight.

"I thank you for the offer, Ethan, really I do. You are sweet, if not a bit unorthodox, but Sedgemoor is not far from Stolford land. I cannot stay here." She placed her hand on his cheek. The blood had now dried where she'd scratched him earlier. "Sorry about that, I normally do not embrace violence."

"What if we were to leave this place together?"

"I cannot ask you to leave your home. I have chosen this life, but I will not entice you to do the same."

"You do nothing to lure me away. I've always known I'd leave Sedgemoor someday. My brother weds in two days. He and Tessa will live at Quesnay. They've invited me to live there, as their captain at arms, but I feel as if that's just trading one form of dependency for another. I'm tired of feeling warm and cozy. Brendan wasn't satisfied with the comfort of mediocrity; neither shall I be."

"Who is Brendan, your brother?"

"A brother of sorts; Aye, we are kin. I am some-what a student of St. Brendan the Navigator's writings. He sailed everywhere! Would Dalibar allow me to travel with the family?"

"He is always open to sojourners, especially those with a strong back," she grinned.

"So, it is settled then? May I have your hand, Mistress Stolford?" he asked as he knelt before her on the battlements.

"Look there; someone's entering the woods," Belinda murmured as she squinted through the spyglass toward forest of trees that dotted Dundrennan.

"Uh, Belinda, *my proposal?*"

Lucian entered the forest with only minutes to spare until the appointed rendezvous time. A rustling to his left told him that his associate had also arrived. *Obviously he hadn't spent much time hunting, the clod thrashes around like a great, clumsy dog,* Lucian sighed.

"Let us be about our business, Baron, I haven't much time."

"I thought you would never get here! There are wee beasties in these woods that unnerve me!" Reginald La Quesnay complained as he brushed dirt from his fur-lined cloak.

"You appear warm enough anyway," Lucian was not sympathetic, "My next assignment will have to be posing as someone of wealth. Gypsies travel too light; I had to leave my warmest things behind."

"Have you found proof of the witchcraft?" Reginald asked as he licked his lips.

"Not as yet, but their priest is nervous. Something is going on here."

"Will he be a problem?" Reginald wanted his castle back with no more delays.

"A young cur who was once my student, actually. He will not stand in my way."

"The wedding is in two days. I want my nephew to suffer. Shall we kill his bride before they say their vows, or do we wait; let them taste real joy, then steal her breath away?" Reginald's eyes began to blaze a most unearthly shade as he debated.

"Control yourself, man. It is a church matter. Let me dispose of her legally. 'Twill not be as enjoyable, I admit, but there can be no recompense this way. After all, the proof will be overwhelming indeed, I guarantee it."

"You know, you and I could've been great friends in other circumstances. You're wicked. I like that in a priest," Reginald laughed.

"I'm not wicked. I just know what I want and I'm willing to do what is required to get it."

"Amen to that. By the way, have you any liquor, so we may drink to our success?" Lucian reached within the folds of his woolen cloak and retrieved another flask of whiskey for his pathetic pawn.

CHAPTER 16

❀

SE RENDRE SACRE'

Early morning brought Jolie from the weaving house with a wrapped parcel for Tessa. She entered the great hall and found Elspeth sipping tea with her daughter.

"Your gown is finished, dear. Shall I take it to your chambers?" Jolie asked.

"It is finished? Thank you so much, Jolie. My only hope is that he won't mind me wearing this dress."

"When he sees you, I'll wager that all other thoughts will fly from his head," Jolie winked at Elspeth.

"Aye, you will be a vision on the morrow. Now take the gown to your room before something happens to it," Elspeth shooed Tessa up the stairs. The mother of the bride turned to the mother of the groom; "We need to talk."

"All right. I promised Artemis I would look in on the observatory while he is away. Walk with me and we can talk on the way," Jolie offered. The staff was scurrying about, preparing the keep for the wedding, as the two women left the front gate and headed toward the river's convergence. Wrapped snugly in their heavy cloaks, both women looked like hooded monks from an English monastery. The light snow from the previous evening crunched under their feet.

"Couldn't we have ridden? Surely Rod would've readied two mounts for us," Elspeth puffed.

"He offered to do so, but I prefer to walk. It's quite cleansing, you know."

"Cleansing?' Elspeth rolled her eyes, *what a loon!*

"In a spiritual sense, I mean of course. I find a good walk clears out the cobwebs," Jolie assured her as they approached the stone bridge spanning the water, "What did you wish to speak to me about?"

"I think I owe you an apology."

"You do? I daresay as the Lady of the castle, you do not owe me, your weaver, anything at all."

"I have resented you for so long, Jolie. It pains me to admit this but I have envied you for years."

"You envy our small cottage and the long hours we work? Nay, I have nothing you could possibly want," Jolie snorted.

"Aye, but you do. You raised a fine son, in Ruffian. He's a man of honor, and that's because of you. And also, you have a kinship with Tessa that I have never shared. She loves me; of course I know that. But she doesn't seek me out to spend time with, like she does with you. I admit that has hurt me a little."

"I am sorry, I didn't know it effected you like that. I never intended to steal your daughter away, Elspeth." Jolie touched her hand, "You shall always be Tessa's mother."

"And you shall always be Ruffian's. La Quesnay or no, he will always be a Bardougne is his heart." An understanding was forged between them as they neared the observatory. The door to the domed tower was never locked, though the second step, once inside, was placed lower than should be, to trip up those who didn't know better. It was Artemis' way of catching strangers from entering his home at night without his knowledge. The few brave souls who had tried to sneak inside for a peek at the timeless treasures he housed, had met with a wicked fall down the rest of the stone steps into the face of Hubert, Artemis' mastiff. Hubert was a huge, slobbering dog with a coat so black; it almost appeared blue in the sunlight. Though he ran free most of the time, he took his naps within the tower. A doggie flap made from wool hung over the custom-made opening in the door. There was no need for a lock. Jolie called for the beast and made soft kissing noises until a great head appeared through the flap.

"There's a good baby," she crooned, "Can we come inside and visit?"

"I think I shall wait outside," Elspeth sputtered at the site of the dog.

"Nonsense! Hubert is a sweet boy, he wouldn't hurt a soul," Jolie said in a sing song voice to ease the beast.

"Why am I not convinced?" Hubert took that moment to shake his huge head and a great spiral of slobber flew in all directions. "Oh, that is just vile!" Elspeth gasped.

"Forget the dog and come in here, I want to show you some things."

The morning light illuminated the walls, as it filtered through the narrow windows to the north. Hubert grumbled a bit at the intrusion, but then settled down on his rug after turning three times in place, as canines are prone to do for some mysterious reason known only to them. A spiraling staircase led to the domed roof, with curved windows that looked upon the sun, moon and the *five wanderers* as he called certain planets. A meticulous record keeper, scrolls and parchments sat in stacks around the remarkable dwelling.

"He certainly is a bit eccentric, isn't he?" Elspeth asked as Hubert began to snore.

"How shall I describe Artemis? He spends his time contemplating the correlation between birdsong and the light filtering through the leaves on a breezy day. He's convinced that when the full moon wanes, it will lose its hold on the raindrops we sometimes pray for on dry summer evenings. He believes in the Trinity, but embraces knowledge as well as faith in the unseen. He is a cultural historian, a healer, a scribe and poet, weaving his visions into the fabric of scientific theory. He was my first friend when I came to Sedgemoor, and I shall always feel great affinity for him. Look, he left me a message," Jolie pointed to the small rough-hewn table near his collection of navigational tools; the astrolabes and quadrants laid covered in a layer fine dust.

∾

My friend,

If you've found this, it means indeed I have been called away. Thank you for checking on things in my absence. Hubert will be fine without me there. He has proven to be most independent. However, it does ease my care to know you are there.

As we experience this life we are given, it sometimes happens that the Mighty One guides us in ways that diverge from those we have shared so much. So it is, for me now. A task has been given into my care from the foundations of time. Being a scribe responsible for the keeping of truths and documenting the history of the 33 messengers has been a heavy weight upon my shoulders. Though I know it is my destiny to be a servant of both God and mankind; of my brothers that ride in unity and purpose. You know well, the brotherhood of which I speak. I cannot fulfill this duty if my heart and mind are with thee, and so I must part from you for a time. It is important work, a sacred duty, and now my hands are free to embrace the task I've been called to complete.

It is my prayer that the Lord will lead me back among your circle again one day, to share wisdom and laughter; truth and tears with those who know me best. You, my dear Jolie, are a weaver in every sense of the word. I thank you for weaving light and love into my existence. Continue weaving hope into this place of safe haven. The world outside Dundrennan is ruthless and cold. Keep the hearth warm, for when my task is done, I shall return. I have left documents I think you should read. It will explain a lot. I hope you will forgive me for keeping the truth from you for so long. 'Tis only of late, I felt the time had truly come for all to be revealed. The 33 are more than legend; more than a mist or shadow you see from the corner of your eye. They are real, living, warrior——priests who traverse this land, and other lands, to protect what is right and true. In your heart, you know them well, and understand their ways because it is also a part of you.

You are my dearest friend,
I shall ever remain your servant,

Artemis

"What is he talking about? That Artemis, sometimes I wonder about him," Elspeth murmured. A thick book of parchments was next to the letter, the cover was of goat hide, and tied with a thin strip of leather that looped over a bone button.

"Obviously, he did not make this book," Jolie said as she opened it, "If he had, 'twould be made from wool or woven grasses." They both smiled.

The first page quoted scripture from the book of Matthew, "Therefore every scribe who has been trained for the kingdom of heaven is like a householder, who brings out of his treasure, what is new and what is old." The next few pages were a genealogy of sorts; though not necessarily of bloodlines. It was a genealogy recording the priesthood of the 33. Dating from 1180; the list of names and places were most astonishing. Flipping through the brittle parchments, they found what was probably the first mention of Dundrennan. The year was 1206. One of the priests, Micah, had brought a group of persecuted believers there to set up a communal sanctuary. Notes were jotted in the record covering the next four years, telling of the planting of orchards and farming the rich soil. It spoke of a power source deep within the ground that seemed to emanate a low-level vibration of some sort. Amantius, a Byzantine, and the scribe at the time, noted that the believers chose the spot where the vibration was the strongest to build their altar to the living God. Other buildings were constructed during that time also. The book spoke of living quarters and stables to hold both livestock and farming tools. Several births and deaths were also listed in the record, though the writing abruptly stopped after the year 1210.

"Do you think we could take this back to Sedgemoor and read it there? I'm beginning to feel uncomfortable here," Elspeth asked.

"Aye, let us get back to the castle. They'll be sending a search party out for us if we do not return soon. God be with you, Hubert. Be a good dog now," Jolie patted Hubert's head as she placed a bit of yellow ribbon in the place where they stopped reading and closed the book. Latching the bone and leather clasp, she tucked the hairy book under her cloak as they left the observatory and headed toward the castle. Hubert raised his great head from his rug just in time to see them close the door. A wide yawn was his only reply.

By the time the women had returned to Sedgemoor, some of the guests had started arriving for the wedding. Meant to be a small affair, there were still those who had to be in attendance outside of the two families and those who lived in and around the castle proper. Charlton Colver, who was a representative from Edward's court, had just arrived to witness the nuptials and report back to the Crown that all was in order. Edward liked to know that all of his demesne were in line and accounted for. Ruffian choosing a bride himself relieved Edward the task of finding a bride for him. As Lady of Sedgemoor, Elspeth rushed to welcome him and to see him to his chamber. Jolie plunked herself down on the leather settee in front of the fire and continued to read from the goat hide book.

The saga picked up again, nearly a generation later. Nathan, a new scribe, related the building of Sedgemoor on the ruins of Se Rendre Sacre', or *Church of the Sacred Surrender*. The MacLures had left intact the orchards and Rhoslefain Abbey, or the *Rose Abbey* as it was often called, that was only partially finished all those years ago. A consecration ceremony took place at the castle, as the last block was laid in place. 'Remembering the faith of those who had gone before, we name this place Sedgemoor, in honor of Brother Micah Sedgemoor, who brought pilgrims here in faith of a new day. To the One who weaves the seas before us and the skies above us, You who weaves our destiny, we bow before Thee and ask Your blessings upon this gathering of we; your servants.'

And at that, Rory MacLure, the first Laird of Sedgemoor, inhabited the land of Dundrennan.

"He was Tormond's grandfather," Jolie nodded.

The book went on to announce the birth of a son, Tormond MacLure; son of Alisdare and Brigid, of Skye, in the year 1264. The babe was celebrated as the first Laird to have been born on the land. Nathan, the scribe, also entered the birth of his own son, Artemis, just 3 days later. To Jolie's surprise, her friend's name appeared in the genealogy of the 33.

"He's one of the brotherhood? How could I have *not* known that?" she whispered as she read by the fire.

"Anything of interest?" Elspeth asked as she bustled into the hall. All her guests were settled in their rooms until the evening meal. That gave her a few hours to relax before jumping again into the role of the gracious hostess.

"You look a bit bewildered, m'lady," Jolie commented, as Elspeth joined her on the settee.

"Oh, well now, we all know why Charlton Colver is here. An agent for the Crown is all he is, which is fine, mind you, but he could at least be up front about it. Why, he went on for nigh an hour about his best wishes for the children; at how wonderful the union of our families will be, blah, blah, blah. Doesn't he realize I have others to tend to?" Elspeth huffed as she bent down to rub her sore feet.

"Mayhap dwelling in the King's shadow gives him little opportunity to feel important."

"Aye, you are probably right," Elspeth nodded as the servants filed into the hall to set for up the night's meal. "So tell me what you have found in that hideous goat book."

"It is getting a bit crowded in here. Are you up to a bit more fresh air?"

"Another trek through the forest?" Elspeth rolled her eyes as she rubbed her feet.

"Nay, just out to the abbey garden."

"Not much growing but boxwood and holly this time of year."

"I wasn't interested in the plant life. The book mentions the abbey many times, there must be something of relevance out there."

"Well, let me get my heavy cloak, it's colder than a witch's…"

"*M'lady!*"

"Well it *is*! Bundle yourself so you don't catch your death before the wedding!" Elspeth commanded. Jolie particularly hated that mothering tone the lady of the keep used on her from time to time. They met at the gate, fully covered in warm woolen robes. Jolie held the fur-covered book next to her chest as they walked. The sun was out. It pierced the snow-laden clouds long enough to let the women know it was still there after all. The trees were frosted a pearlescent white. The same magical frost adorned the iron gate of the abbey, in a filigree of tiny, splintering designs.

"Leave the gate open," Elspeth said as Jolie moved to close it behind them.
"Why?"
"Because I don't like feeling locked in."
"M'lady, the walls are not even intact. You can see the trees and sky all around you."
"The gate remains open," she snapped.
"As you wish," Jolie mumbled something under her breath about a bad humor in the blood causing nobles to go mad.
"Tell me what this book says."
"Well, it chronicles the history of two families; of sorts; the MacLures, as they relate to the land of Dundrennan, and another family; the 33. Even some of our own guards are of that group." Elspeth nodded, unsure she wanted to hear the rest.
"The genealogy in this book relates a story from near Biblical times. There were a group of followers who were dispersed after the crucifixion, to far-off lands. The group numbered 33 in all, to mark to number of years our Lord walked the earth. Each made a solemn oath to uphold and defend all that is right in the world, and to defend the weak and needy by any means necessary. Mercy was great but judgment was swift and terrible. They formed a warrior-priesthood that was to remain secret, lest Rome would hunt them down as followers of the Christ, and martyr them as they had several others in that day. One of the 33 was Simeon, or Simon the brother of Jesus; son of Mary. Though the others were of rather mundane descent, it was decided that membership in the 33 would be inherited. The bloodline was to travel through the *mother's line*, as Mary was of the tribe of Judah and in the lineage of King David. The priests were encouraged to marry and have children, but only those who displayed obvious gifts of discernment or strength of character would inherit a place in the 33," Jolie read aloud as she flipped the brittle parchments.
"That is all very interesting, but what has that to do with us?" Elspeth was getting cold waiting for some point to the excursion into the snow.

"I do not know. However I *did* find Artemis' name among the 33, look!" Jolie pointed to the listing.

"Good for him. Can we go now?" Elspeth glanced at the book Jolie was shoving in her face, just to appease the woman. "Oh my word, that cannot be right. My father's name is listed there."

"Where!" Jolie's eyes widened, *I knew there was a reason behind all this!* She followed Elspeth's trembling finger down the list to William Essex, born October 25th, 1248; the son of Theobold Essex and Madelynn Celestine. The Celestine name appeared on the list from very early on.

"*Someday that name will mean something to you*," Elspeth mumbled, remembering Alasdair's words so long ago.

"Of course the name William Essex means something to me!" Jolie shouted at her mistress, "He is my father!"

"You lie." Elspeth's eyes became cold and darker as she looked upon the weaver. "I am the daughter of William Essex and Margaret Bell."

"I know no Margaret, but my father is William Essex! I was born in France, the daughter of William Essex and Celeste Aubergine. I lived with them until I married Rod and came to live here at Sedgemoor," Jolie insisted.

"My father left me here alone at the age of eight summers," Elspeth spat as tears streamed down her face.

"Why did he leave?"

"You tell me."

"Are you saying I knew about all this?"

"Why then did you end up *here*, of all places?" Elspeth accused.

"This was Rod's home. His work was here!" Jolie defended.

"Did *your father* know where Rod hailed from?"

"I suppose so; after all, I doubt he'd let me run off God-knows where!"

"And did he seem supportive of your move so far away?"

"He always supported me," Jolie whispered, "He loved me."

"That must be a nice feeling!" she spat.

"This has got to be a mistake. Someone entered the wrong name in these records."

"Wrong or not, what are the chances of our fathers having the same name?" Elspeth was numb, "So he went to France after my mother died. Alisdare said it was because he was *overcome* with grief. A change of scenery would do him good, I was told. Didn't he think I could use a change as well?" Elspeth cried, "I watched my mother die before my eyes. I felt her cold body as I tried over and over to wake her. Didn't he think I'd want to rid myself of those nightmares?

All I wanted was to be with him, but he didn't care. I remember the day he rode away from me and never looked back."

"I never knew. I swear I never knew any of this," Jolie whispered. She wanted to comfort her sister, but how? Jolie had had her father's love and company her whole life. He was a man of music and tales. He was always laughing. *How could he have had another life?*

Elspeth had run onto the path of the ancient prayer labyrinth that was inlaid upon the abbey floor. Time and neglect had forced the abbey to surrender to nature, as an abundance of plant life, now dormant from winter's touch, had turned the church into a walled garden. The center of the labyrinth still boasted an altar. Jolie followed Elspeth on the winding path, pleading for her to stop. A swirling breeze surrounded them as they delved deeper and deeper into the spiraling path. A whooshing sound filled both their minds and they had the queer sense of movement, like being carried by an unseen hand to another place. They reached out for one another without thinking. As before at Tessa's sickbed, the sisters were given a vision of the past. Elspeth's parents were dancing on Michaelmas; William held a tiny Elspeth in his arms as he swayed with his wife. The 33 were riding across the hills in pursuit of truth. Margaret's death; Elspeth crying and William drinking outside the cottage. The 33 standing vigil near Margaret's grave. William giving his daughter a brooch that had belonged to *his* mother, then riding away forever. Jolie's birth; her mother, Celeste, screaming out as their daughter entered the world. William down on his knees under a canopy of stars, praying before sending a parchment on with a lone rider; one of the 33 bound for Sedgemoor. Jolie learning to weave at her mother's knee. Her father walking her to Rod on their wedding day. William giving her a pendant in token and gift to remember him by. His face as he watched her leave his life, to go to Sedgemoor; where he had left his heart all those years ago.

The whooshing sound grew to an unbearable pitch until abruptly, it stopped. The two women nearly fell, as the power of the vision released them. Night had fallen. The stars of a millennia twinkled down upon them. The sky was as dark as rich, indigo velvet. Speechless, the two found themselves at the center of the labyrinth. Jolie placed her pendant upon the altar and looked at her sister; the one person who could vex her more than any other. Elspeth reached inside her cloak and brought forth the brooch she'd received so long ago. Opals of matching depth and size shone back at them in the moonlight.

"It is their mark," Jolie mumbled incoherently.

"What?"

"In the book, it talks about the opal as the mark of the 33. *'Fire in the sky, fire in the stone, fire in the rainbow, marks our brotherhood,'* she recited from memory. The vision had not only given them a look at past events that linked them together; they had also felt deeply the love and pain of all that had been involved. Understanding and forgiveness once again washed over them as they embraced.

"A most interesting evening indeed." Lucian grinned as he walked silently away from the open iron gate of Rose Abbey.

Lucian Medieros spent the night wandering the bowels of the castle in search of the treasure he'd heard rumor of. He found the natural spring that fed fresh water directly into the castle. The damp, cool stones surrounding the indoor well were covered with a soft green film of moss-like plant life. Lucian sat on the edge and peered into the water. The image staring back at him was indeed evil embodied. *When had he changed?*

I knew I was destined to be so much more than a farmer's son. My ambition was respected in seminary. They said I had drive, and determination. They had no idea what it was I really wanted... The papacy? What a joke! Too much attention, and not near enough privacy to indulge my taste for life's little pleasures. No, I can use my position to move in and out of the church's objectives to suit my own agendas. No one questions a man of the cloth; it's the perfect arrangement. And I will have my way. I'll find this legendary treasure and then leave a little something for these idiots to remember me by. Lucian's teeth gleamed even brighter in the torch light, as he smiled at himself in the liquid mirror. After one last glance around the tidy, but dank chamber, he spit in the well and disappeared into another darkened corridor.

The next day no one even missed Michelassi in all the traffic of preparing both for the Christmas Eve feast and the wedding on Christmas day. Reginald had kept his part of the devil's bargain. He hovered in the tree line near Sedgemoor with a poor soul who had been forced to bear witness against the MacLures, out of fear for his own life. Reginald had him tied to a tree and gagged with a wad of flaxen cloth. He waited for Lucian for hours but the priest never came. He'd been without liquor for nearly four days, and every nerve in his body seemed to be on fire.

"Where the hell is he?" Reginald cursed to his prisoner. The poor man only could manage a shoulder shrug in answer. Reginald curled his cut and chapped hands into tight fists to keep them from shaking uncontrollably. He licked his cracked lips in anticipation of more whiskey from his benefactor. *Soon Quesnay will be mine again. The priest will ruin the MacLures and shame them from Dundrennan, and I will see Raphael's demise myself, with pleasure!*

Lucian entered the confessional just after two women from the weaving house exited. The two watched him with interest, as they had never imagined that Gypsies went to confession. Bryan slid open the portal used to hear the bearings of tortured souls, only to see his mentor staring back at him clad in the garish clothes of the travelers.

"Have you found anything against the MacLures?" Bryan asked in a whisper.

"Do not concern yourself with the details, Delyth. Let me ask you something. Have you ever seen the women conjure spirits or speak in the course of a vision?"

"Nay, Father, never!"

"Well it might interest you to know that indeed, I have witnessed such demonic practice myself this very night. The Lady of the keep was consorting with that weaver woman in some satanic ritual, right inside that pile of rubble you call an abbey. What sacrilege! What evil runs rampant here!"

"Nay you must be mistaken, Father. I know these people! They are believers!" Bryan pleaded.

"You are calling me a liar?" Lucian seethed with secret hate for the pure heart before him.

"Nay, only you misunderstood what you saw, sir," Bryan backed down.

"As God as my witness, I know what I saw, Delyth. Now you can stand with me; and live to see yourself promoted and possibly even moved to serve in Avignon itself, or…" The silence filled the chamber like a lead weight pulling Bryan down into the depths of Lucian's wicked plan. "…you will see first hand the awesome fury of God's wrath upon this hold."

"I cannot testify to what I do not know, Father. Do what you must, and I shall do the same. And may God have mercy on us both." Bryan closed the portal to his future, his past, and the delusion that his hero could never fall from grace.

Jolie sat curled up on a chair close to her hearth. Their cottage smelled so richly of fine leather tack, peat smoke, and bundles of dyed yarn drying by the fire. She opened her private journal and began to write.

∾

Holy One,

The energy is real, I feel it throughout Dundrennan. I knew the minute I came here, that You were here too. And I know there were others. Long ago, faithful souls who loved You, and sought out a place; a special niche in the hills to seek Your favor. I can almost picture them praying under the trees, or walking the labyrinth in silence. I can see them washing away the dust of the day in the streams that flow on forever.

These fields were once theirs, to feed the poor. We built upon the remnants, where families once dwelt. Surely not all were extinguished, like a candle snuffed out in the darkness. There's a pull to this land, like a soul-magnet that draws us here and keeps us.

I can sometimes hear their prayers. I feel them encircle, and call out Your name; Holy One, Abba Father, Savior, King. As sure as I breathe, I know You delivered them. Somehow, some way, You gathered Your own.

May we who follow, be faithful to what was started so long ago.

CHAPTER 17

❀

A GATHERING OF HEARTS

Christmas Day, 1309

Christmas morn dawned clear and bright over the frosty moors of Dundrennan. Tessa's chamber was filled with harried women as they poked, prodded, teased, cinchedand laced Tessa up like a holiday goose. Jolie had altered Journey's gown to fit Tessa as if it had been custom made for her alone. The women stood back and admired their handiwork. A tear slipped down Belinda's cheek, as her thoughts drifted to Ethan and the life they could never have together. His proposal had been so sudden, but she could think of nothing else since their time alone on the battlements.

"Belinda, is everything all right? Are you unwell?" Tessa asked.

"I am well, 'tis only the excitement of the day," she murmured.

"'Tis Ethan, isn't it? That boy can stir up such a commotion! Do you know once when we were small, he put cow dung in my braids? 'Tis true! Ruffian blackened his eye over it, but I think only because he hadn't thought of the prank himself." Belinda laughed in spite of her misery. "In truth, I see you care for him. He is a mischievous sort, but a more loyal heart you shall never find. Belinda, if it's one thing I've learned, it is to trust my instincts; my heart. Please promise me you will do the same." Elspeth touched Tessa on the sleeve as Belinda left the chamber, "What was that all about?"

"Just paying back a debt, mother," she grinned.

Tormond stalked back and forth in front of the stone fireplace in the great hall. The massive Yule log blazed, sending beads of sweat down his back. The horses were waiting. Rod had braided holly into Lachlan's golden mane and polished Tessa's saddle. All was ready.

"Damnation, where is that girl?" Tormond boomed.

A gloved hand gently touched the Laird's mighty arm.

"Be at peace, father, I am right here." One look at his daughter and all impatience fled.

"Are ye ready, my sweet girl?" he gruffed with false bravado.

"He is all I have ever wanted, father." Her smile stole his breath away. *So like Elspeth at that age, but with a light all her own.* She was stunning in the pale blue gown; tiny pearls and diamonds dripping from the hem and neckline, like tiny icicles, and her small satin-slippered foot was tapping impatiently beneath the glittering hem.

Ruffian rode Thunder across the moors to claim what had, in truth, always been his. They all gathered beneath the Ancient Oak on the hill. Impressed by the number of well-wishers there, he dismounted and handed the reins to Rod.

"Treat her well, lad, or I'll have to hunt you down and thrash you."

"I love you too, father." The two embraced roughly as men often do; not wanting to seem over emotional. He looked over the moors and spotted Tessa and her father riding toward the gathering. Her hair was already coming down from her braid. He smiled at all the times he'd seen that happen. He found himself holding his breath as he watched her. A carriage followed behind with Elspeth, Jolie and Serrah.

With everyone settled around the ancient tree, Father Bryan began the ceremony. The old Scottish custom of exchanging Bibles was observed. Each one, with their family lineage scrolled lovingly inside, signified the union of two families into one. Simple vows spoken; allegiances sworn beneath the tree, all with the promise to remain true "until we see heaven". And one more miracle had been wrought beneath the Oak of Dundrennan.

After many hugs and well wishes, the marriage supper was held. All the villagers were invited to partake of the food and warmth from the MacLure hearth. Dalibar's travelers provided the music, the ale and wine from Sedgemoor's stores allowed the party to flow into the deepening night. No one seemed to notice the beggar, clothed in dingy woolen rags, crouched near the stairway. He had been tired of waiting in the woods for Lucian. He left his "witness" tied to the tree and slipped into the castle with the other guests. The smell of food and wine was almost his undoing. Reginald watched the gypsies dance and sing, but never caught sight of the priest. His empty silver flask was mocking him from the folds of his tattered cloak.

"Damn that man, to leave me freezing in the woods while he's here, warm, fed and dry!" Reginald grumbled, "I will not be so easily dismissed."

As everyone was dancing in the great hall, Lucian made his way through the crowd. He'd searched for two days with nothing to show for his efforts. He brushed by Tormond as he and Elspeth danced. The Laird noticed traces of light green on Lucian's leggings. A bushy eyebrow cocked ever so slightly as the gypsy passed by and smiled. A ragged hand shot out and grabbed him as soon as he entered the outer corridor.

"You think to disregard your dealings with me?" Reginald slurred. He had found a way to secure a horn of fine Scottish whiskey while he'd been waiting.

"You pathetic excuse for a man, get your filthy hands off me," Lucian warned.

"Or what? You'll call the guards? Oh, let's do that, shall we? I have loads to tell the Laird."

"You despise the MacLures. You won't do that."

"Ah yes, but as it turns out, I think I hate you more. So, I figure I have nothing to lose and everything to gain by becoming Tormond's new confidante. I will save them from the likes of you, making me a hero! My nephew will forgive and forget, maybe set me up in a nice country house near Quesnay. We will spend holidays together, one big happy family."

"Here, have another drink," Lucian handed Reginald a tankard of ale, "we need to talk."

Blessings and toasts were bestowed upon the couple. Jolie had finally come to terms with her son's new life. Rod gave her shoulders a good squeeze before heading off toward the smoked pig and butternut squash soup. The soup was actually a concoction that Rod and cook made together. He loved to cook, and only his wife knew that the secret ingredient was a healthy shot of ale to give the soup its whollop.

"My pardon, Mistress Bardougne, but might I speak with you in private?" Father Delyth asked quietly.

"Of course, Father." They slipped into the study where they would not be disturbed, a muffled voice and hurried shuffle brought Ethan and Belinda from behind one of the heavy tapestries that hung low on one wall. Ethan was beginning to blush, with the red starting at the base of his neck and traveling up his face by the time they reached the door leading back to the party.

"What can I do for you, Father?" she asked, hoping he would disregard what he just saw her son doing.

"God forgive me, but I fear I have brought great ruin to Sedgemoor."

"Surely not you, Father, you are of gentle spirit and I see how you love the MacLures."

"Know you, the gypsy named Michalassi?" he squirmed.

"Aye, I know who he is. Why?" Jolie began to feel a familiar sickening knot forming in her stomach. *There is a storm on the horizon,* she cringed.

"He is not who he says he is. He is a priest sent here by the Bishop to weed out heretics."

"There be no heretics here," Jolie assured him.

"I tried to tell him as much, but he's heard rumors of…" he looked away.

"Rumors of what?" she pressed him, already knowing what he was going to say. "They think we practice the Old Religion, do they not?"

"Aye, they do. And Father Medieros is looking for some cursed treasure that the MacLures supposedly stole from their homeland."

"Well, I know nothing of a treasure, but there are people who would testify to our gifts of sight, if the price was high enough. How do you know this man?"

"I am ashamed to say he was my teacher, my mentor as I studied for the priesthood."

"Is he truly in the service of the church?"

"Nay, I believe he has lost sight of his calling and gone off seeking his own glory. He is not the man I once knew. He is bitter now, angry, power-hungry. I mourn the loss of such a servant as he. His priesthood gave me mine, but no longer. The man I knew is dead and this monster reigns within him. I know not what to do to stop him." Bryan held up his hands in surrender.

"You have done all you could. Now go on about your duties to this family. I shall handle things from here." Jolie gave the young priest a quick hug of thanks and left to find Tormond.

Lucian had led Reginald into a seldom-used sitting room and gave him another drink.

"What information do you have for me?" he asked the drunken man.

"I found one man willing to testify against the MacLure girl, for a price. It seems she refused his attentions on more than one occasion and he has a bit of a score to settle. He requires a new set of clothes and 10 pieces of silver in order to tell his story." Reginald burped, then smiled.

"Fool! He would be easily dismissed! No one would believe a scorned lover or whatever the creature is! Where is he, anyway?"

"Oh, you'll be happy to know he's still out in the woods tied to a tree. I couldn't let him get away, now could I?"

"And how often do you suppose the Sedgemoor guards walk the grounds looking for intruders, especially on this, the Laird's daughter's wedding?" Lucian's voice was a mere hiss,

"If he is found, he'll spill everything and you, my friend, will be a dead man."

"What about you?" Reginald offered.

"Me? I am only a base-born troubadour. Your witness knows nothing of me," he sneered.

"Ah, I am afraid he does. Well, the hours dragged on, and you never came back! I had to talk to someone! He was very impressed with your plan to ruin the MacLures, he really was! I say, have you any more ale?" Lucian left Reginald sitting in the darkened room mumbling incoherently to himself.

A half an hour later, the guards found the mutilated torso of a man tied to a tree. He looked as if wolves had made dinner of him, yet they wondered how he came to be tied up. No one could recognize the man's face as most of it had been cut away but some crazed monster. Lucian had lost track of Reginald amidst the sea of wedding guests that were still dancing and feasting. A woman, one of the survivors of the massacre in the village of Thierry pressed against Lucian in the crowd. She lost her footing and grabbed his collar to catch herself from falling. In the commotion she managed to pull his cross from his neck. Horror spread across her face as she remembered the man who had lead the attack against her village. He was dressed in priest's garb and the garish bejeweled cross glimmered in the firelight of their burning homes. Jolie had witnessed the exchange between the gypsy and the woman. She had looked for Tormond, but could not seem to locate the man. Lucian disappeared into the crowd and Jolie helped the poor woman.

"He is the devil, he is!" she cried. She proceeded to tell Jolie her tale.

Blessings and toasts were bestowed upon the couple. Tessa unveiled her special gift to Ruffian. At first he thought it was supposed to be her, *but the hair is all wrong.* Then she explained about the day at Quesnay, and what she had found. She decided to leave out the part about the portrait being slashed. At that, Reginald nearly went mad. *I thought the wench looked familiar.* Now seeing the portrait had brought it all horribly back to him.

"It is the whore Adrian took for his wife! I thought I destroyed that cursed painting! How did she get a hold of it? Mayhap, 'tis true, she is a witch of the old religion!" he mumbled. The voices were screaming at him now. He shook his head to make them stop, but they called on and on.

While the dancing continued, Ruffian discreetly stole his bride away. Up the winding staircase to her tower chamber, he carried her in his arms. In all the excitement, Tessa's stomach had not been in the mood for food. The wine was catching up with her as she snuggled contentedly against her husband's chest. He pushed the chamber door open with his foot to reveal a four poster bed, which had been moved there just after the ceremony had begun. Her room had been turned into a fantasy bridal chamber. The bed itself, in rich mahogany, was clad in soft, white furs. A fire blazed in the stone hearth that bathed the room in a warm glow. Beeswax candles shone all around, filling the room with a sweet, seductive scent that tempted and teased their senses.

He placed her most reverently upon their bed. He knelt before here and reached under the hem of her gown. As her breath quickened at her husband's touch, she felt him caress her calves as he slowly removed her satin slippers.

"Be right back," he whispered and kissed her forehead.

"Wh…What?" she slurred. The minutes seemed like hours as she waited for his return. She lay back on the furs and closed her eyes. The fire soon lulled her into a wonderful sleep. Moments later she awoke to being carried once more. She grinned crookedly and hiccuped. But this was not Ruffian. He did not feel the same, or smell the same as he had moments before. Tessa's eyes shot open and her body tensed as she realized she was being taken somewhere without her permission, by someone other than her husband. She winced at his foul breath and struggled not to gag. She tried to relax and get a glimpse of exactly where they were in the castle. They were still in the tower, but they continued up toward the battlements on the roof. She feigned a swoon until they reached the top and the creature unceremoniously dumped her in a heap upon the flat roof.

He backed away from her then. He pulled out his refilled flask and drank long from the liquid fire within. She watched as he stumbled to the edge and looked out over the moors. She got to her feet and lightly felt down the length of her left thigh. There, beneath the thick blue satin, was Ruffian's gift to her, Journey's dagger. Reginald turned and began to swear before heaven and earth that it was his duty to rid the place of witches and whores.

"A thankless job, but someone has to do it!" he reasoned, *What? Did no one understand that?* He held his trembling hand to his temple and squeezed his eyes shut against the pain.

"No, no no! Not *that way!*" he screamed…to…no one.

Tessa realized who the madman was. The feast was still going on in the hall far below. The music drifted happily up to the battlements. No one would hear her screams. She knew that no one knew where she was. It would be up to her to deal with Reginald herself. He turned again and stepped to the edge. Draining his flask, he let out a curse and flung it over the battlements to the courtyard below. Tessa lay hold of the dagger and slipped it free from her garter. She held it steady within the folds of her gown. Breathing a prayer for wisdom and help, she stepped forward.

"Reginald! How dare you come here, where you drove me to my death?" Tessa stepped forward. His eyes widened as he saw Journey coming closer. He knew that he would meet her again someday.

"Be gone, foul spirit!" he yelped and stepped back, dangerously close to the roof's edge. *That's it. He thinks I am Journey,* she smiled. It was her only hope.

Ruffian stepped back into the chamber to find nothing except a few tussled furs upon a now empty bed. A call from the hall caught his attention.

"M'lord, a most curious thing has happened. One of the guards in the courtyard reported that this dropped from the sky! He handed Ruffian the dented flask. It bore the La Quesnay crest. Ruffian had seen Reginald take it with him when he left Quesnay castle.

"Blast and damnation, he has Tessa!" Ruffian growled, "It fell in the courtyard, you say?"

"Aye, m'lord."

"Gather your men. Summon the archers. Ascend the adjacent tower, to the roof. Fire only at my command. He has my wife, I want no mistakes!" and Ruffian was racing up the turret stairs.

"Why don't people I kill just *stay* dead?" he pleaded with her, shaking his head in frustration.

"Because, Reginald, you should not be killing them in the first place!" she scolded.

"How about falling down the stairs? It worked for my mother!" he smiled, "Or mayhap you would like something flashier? Poison? Beheading? I can do them all, you know." He stepped toward her. He traced her jaw line with a gnarled, trembling finger. It lightly trailed down her slender neck and brushed the top of one breast. "Pity, really, I would have so enjoyed you."

Ruffian nudged the turret door open enough to see his Uncle touching his bride. He restrained his anger, knowing one stupid move could prove fatal for Tessa. Reginald circled around her, talking and laughing as if someone else was there.

"A leap? Yes, a leap to her death on her wedding night, how delicious!" he smiled. He pushed her toward the edge of the roof. Ruffian could see the archers assembled on the adjacent tower, ready on his command.

Tessa knew the roof very well. Though warned over and over again, not to play there, it was just above her bedchamber. And, as usual, Tessa listened to her father dutifully, then did as she pleased most of the time. She knew that the third outcropping of stone to the left was loose. The mortar was nearly washed away by the rains that fell across the moors. *If I could just manage to move him in that direction,* she thought.

Reginald babbled on incoherently, confusing Tessa and Journey as he spoke. *He is completely insane,* she was sure of it. She agreed with everything that he said, moving him to the left ever so slightly. Ruffian knew of the loose stone too. He saw what she was doing. She still had no idea that he was there, or that the guard was ready to save her. He held up his hand to stay the guard. In silence he watched on. She didn't want to kill him. She couldn't imagine plunging a blade into a living creature and watching his life drain away. Her hands were sweating, though she tried to remain calm. *God will help me,* she knew it to be true. As he grabbed her arms to pull her forward, he felt the knife in her hand. His eyes flashed green in the moonlight.

"You thought to kill me, wench? Me?" he actually sounded insulted.

He grabbed her wrist. His grip crushing her finely-knit bones. She was sure her hand would break as they twisted and struggled. Just as she thought she could bear the pain no longer, a blinding flash of light streaked smoothly across the winter sky. She ducked and rolled as Reginald covered his eyes. As he lost his balance, he clutched frantically at the battlement. But the stone he clung to was the third outcropping to the left. For a moment, time stopped. Reginald glared at her in disbelief. She looked upon him with pity, as one would a rabid dog who must be destroyed to end its own misery, and for the safety of others. He was a tortured soul, and she was sorry for that. He grasped and clawed to get a better hold, but the large stones were coming loose all around him. He fell in slow motion, it seemed. His scream was hideous. The thud was sickening. She hoped that in those final seconds, Reginald had cried out for God's mercy, for God alone had the power to forgive.

Ruffian rushed through the doorway and pulled her to him.

"Darling, I cannot breathe!" a muffled voice squeaked. He set her away from his chest just enough to look her in the eyes. She was shaking then, as reality set in. The dead man in the courtyard brought both sets of parents and most of the guard running up the turret stairs to see what had happened.

"He thought I was your mother," she said simply. "I am not sure if he loved her or hated her."

"I know," Ruffian replied, holding her once more. "Let me take you inside, Tessa." Both families gathered back in Tessa's chamber as she was given a warm mixture of milk, honey and cinnamon, to calm her. Ethan came crashing in, raving about the comet that had raced across the sky a few moments earlier, "How I wish Artemis was here!"

Lucian had missed the theatrics, but he still managed a slow smile as he stepped across the body in the courtyard and sauntered back to his bed in the stables.

❀

CHAPTER 18

VENGENCE IS MINE

Everyone was falling all over Tessa, making sure she was all right after the events of the night before. Ruffian could see the pleading in her eyes. *I have to get her out of here for awhile*, he decided.

"Lady La Quesnay and I are going to take a ride this morning," he announced, "I would request some privacy so we may dress."

"Are you daft?" Elspeth sputtered.

"Nay, the fresh air will do her good. It's very cleansing."

"So I hear." Elspeth rolled her eyes at Jolie who was grinning broadly.

"She may go, on one condition, young Baron," Elspeth said, "that a guard accompanies you."

"Oh come now, think you I cannot protect my wife?"

"She is our daughter, and my husband outranks you." Elspeth knew she had won by the resigned look upon his face.

"Where are you taking me, m'lord," Tessa asked her husband as they rode toward the river and not to the moors, as usual.

"Mother had a book to return to Artemis, so I volunteered to deliver it and check on Hubert.

"That dog! He is a great, slobbering hound, isn't he?" she laughed as they rode on. It occurred to her that this might be the last time she looked upon the landscape of Dundrennan for a very long time. They approached Artemis' stone tower to Hubert's half-hearted barking. His great, wagging tale betrayed his deep growls and snorts. Ruffian pulled fresh venison from his satchel and threw it to the mastiff, which dragged it under some bushes and began to feast away.

"Watch that second step," Ruffian told her as they entered the observatory that was Atremis' safe haven.

"Aye, I know. About twisted my ankle on it once!" Ruffian placed the goat hair book in an empty space on the bookshelf that spiraled up the stairs. The next volume over caught his eye, *Se Rendre Sacre, Rhoslefain.*

"Tessa, remember the day in the abbey when we were wondering about the people who built it?"

"Who started to build it, you mean? Aye, I remember."

"I think I might have found something here." He handed her an enormous volume clad in leather. She laid it on the table and opened it. Dust motes danced in the morning light from the ancient parchments.

"It is written in French. The beginning date is 1100. The Church of the Sacred Surrender started in France it says, and it looks as though they came here nearly 100 years later, in fear for their lives from religious persecution."

"I can imagine! I am sure they were looked upon as heretics," he nodded.

"Oh my, yes. They believed in such things as women in ministry, a non-celibate priesthood, communal living, controlling the number of babes to be born, among other things," she read.

"Other things? That is enough to have them all burnt!"

"I fear the worst was that they sought to do away with the feudal system. They believed in equality for all; widows, orphans, beggars included."

"The upper-crust of society would never allow that!"

"Nor would the crown or the papacy," Tessa mused.

"Their list of enemies just got larger."

"It sure did." Tessa flipped to the back of the book to see how it ended for the mysterious Church. There were still a few blank pages. The last one with writing was dated in the summer of 1209. It talked about the orchard and the prospect of having a fine harvest to feed all the poor that lived in the village. It mentioned the construction of the 'new abbey', and how lovely it would be for their prayer services. A loose parchment tumbled out from the back of the book. This was written in crude French; a poem or song, Tessa was not sure.

We know it won't be long now. The soldiers are everywhere.
They don't even try to sneak up on us,

But boldly march, their drums beating, like an executioner's song.
The children are so scared. We try to hush their cries,
To give them the courage, to go to God.
The buildings are on fire now.
They've trampled our fields.
There will be no food to feed the poor, after we are gone.
If I'm not afraid to die, then why am I trembling?
In my heart, I am a lion ~ but my body is cold and weak
And scared.
Take us soon ~ That we will endure this madness no longer.
I pray that our faith will not be erased from the earth completely;
That a remnant shall remain to tell the truth ~
To tell of our lives here.
All is not lost.
That is hope's cry.

"They were massacred, every one of them," Ruffian whispered.

"Even the children!" Tessa sobbed, "What wickedness has been wrought on this earth, in the name of religion."

"Aye but the truth *has* survived, for it is here in our hands! Artemis is a scribe, as was his ancestors before him. They have kept the pledge to record and house the truths of this land."

"Yes! And the scribe must have survived the attack because this *Hope's Cry* is here in the records. It had to be added later, after the attack."

"Mayhap because they were wise enough *not* to leave the records with one of their own. Did your mother tell you what they found in the goat hair book?" he asked.

"That Artemis is one of the 33? Aye, she did. I thought they were only a bit of lore."

"That is what they want everyone to think. Is that all she told you?"

"Nay. I found out that we are *quasi-cousins*. And as it turns out, my grandfather was one of the messengers too."

"Aye, and the same man is Ethan's grandfather. That makes Ethan the next in line."

"Hmmm, he doesn't exactly seem the warrior-priestly type," Tessa grinned. Ruffian only smiled, "I think we have yet to see the man that Ethan will become."

The day after Christmas was a busy one for the staff of Sedgemoor. While the Yule celebration would continue on until Epiphany, most of the visitors were making their way back to their homes. Jolie and Elspeth scurried around the keep making sure all was in order. Faint strains of music could still be heard in the great hall, from Dalibar and the travelers. They knew they would soon be expected to move on, but Dalibar had been grateful for the few days' respite that accompanying Belinda Stolford had afforded them.

Lucian had found no treasure in the castle. It had all been for nothing. He could find nothing concrete to charge the MacLures for. No one in or around Sedgemoor would ever testify to heresy. No one alive knew who he really was except for Bryan Delyth, and Lucian believed Bryan's hero-worship of his past mentor would still his tongue. He would simply leave with the gypsies and then disappear all together, to go back to his priestly duties. *The Bishop will not be pleased,* he thought, *but I can blame that drunken sot, La Quesnay, for it all.* The music was just ending as Jolie made her way to the hall. Tormond had been the traveler's only guest at the private concert. His eyes met Jolie's in a moment of silent communication.

"I say, may I have a moment of your time, Michelassi?" Tormond asked Lucian.

"I am at your service, m'lord." Tormond led Lucian to his study, where Jolie was sitting with the woman from Thierry.

"Sit down," the Laird commanded.

"If this is about us moving on, I assure you we were just about to..."

"Why were you in our cellars?"

"I do not know what you are speaking of," the priest lied.

"Look at your leggings, man. The green that is dried there is from the moss growing on our inner cistern. The moss grows no where else at Sedgemoor. I know it well." Tormond explained, "The question remains why were you there?"

"The castle is so big, I must have turned left when I should've turned right."

"Nay, not good enough. I am sure you did not find whatever it was you were looking for. I believe you have met Mistress Bardougne, but do you know this woman?" Lucian knew immediately it was the woman from the wedding feast who had grabbed his cross.

"She looks familiar, but alas I have met so many new people here, I cannot readily remember." Father Bryan quietly entered the study and sat down. He swallowed hard as Lucian glared at him. Bryan could not meet his eyes.

"I shall make this quick. We know who you are, *Father*. Although why the church decided to target us, I am unclear on. No matter, what with the eyewitness we have here, who will swear it was you and your men who decimated the village of Thierry. That would be enough for me just to turn you over to the survivors for justice. But I also know you seek to bring false charges of witchery upon, both my wife, my daughter, and my sister in law. There are no grounds for the charges, and as a man of the cloth, you should know full well the hell that awaits one who would falsely accuse the brethren."

"I planned to do no such thing!" Lucian swore.

"Aye, but you did," Bryan finally spoke.

"You are mistaken," he seethed.

"Let me make this simple, Medeiros, you drop all thought to these ridiculous charges and never set foot on Sedgemoor land again, and in return, we promise you no recompense, and you shall see safe passage back to the Bishop," Tormond offered.

"I was only doing my job. It was nothing personal."

"Aye and that is what is so horrible about you. You slaughtered dozens, mayhap hundreds of people, and it was never *personal*. You derive some perverse pleasure from killing the weak, and you call it *spiritual cleansing?* You are a rouge. Your days as a priest are over. I've already sent a runner with the news for the Archbishop. *Lucian Medeiros has left the ministry. This meeting is over. You have but an hour to be off my land. Leave or die, 'tis up to you.*"

He knew when he had been beat. Lucian gathered his meager belongings from the stables and was leaving Sedgemoor when he heard a noise coming from the old rose abbey. He slipped inside the open gate to see who was there. Serrah was happily making snow angels in the newly fallen Christmas snow. She was singing as she merrily swooshed her woolen-clad arms and legs. Leaving would've been so easily, but Lucian felt the familiar gnawing of untamed lust as he gazed upon the little girl.

"I did promise to leave them something to remember me by," he grinned.

Ethan had the most incredible talk with his parents. Jolie explained about Elspeth and how God had led Jolie there to rejoin the fractured family. She told him of the legacy of the 33 Messengers and gave him the opal that had been her father's.

"I am no priest, mother."

"Priests are not perfect; they are mere men with a vision and a duty, 'tis all."

"Mother, Belinda and I are getting serious."

"Posh, you barely know her."

"Can we discuss this matter later?" Ethan asked, "I'm feeling a bit ill and I need some fresh air." Ethan left his parents and stepped out into the feathery white snow. It seemed to blanket the countryside in purity. He breathed deep, the crisp winter air. He let it fill his lungs to capacity. He held it for as long as he could before slowly letting it out. A modicum of tension left him. He looked out over the snow-capped landscape and sighed, *If it is all so beautiful, why do I want to leave?*

He noticed a set of footprints leading out of the castle grounds, *two sets*, actually. Both led to the abbey, the disappeared. A prickling sensation went up from his neck to his eyebrows. He rubbed his eyes to remove the feeling but it persisted. He hurriedly made his way into the abbey garden. Far in the center of the garden maze, he heard a muffled scream. Something welled up inside him that seemed to just take over at that point. He raced through the maze, for he too, knew its paths well. There on the altar in the center of the maze, Lucian had Serrah. He was on top of her, trying to still the squirming child. In one fluid move, Ethan picked Lucian up by his collar and slammed him against the crumbling stone wall of the abbey.

"Ethan!"

"Go home, Serrah! Now!"

"No, he will hurt you!" she cried.

"Do as I say, girl! Go home and stay there!" The little girl ran straight back to her squat cottage, not far from the castle. The monster had not done the deed; Ethan had interrupted in time.

"You bastard!" Ethan tightened the grip on Lucian's neck.

"Only after a little harmless fun. She's a servant's whelp, it doesn't matter."

"You are right, none of it matters now," Ethan hissed.

"What are you going to do? Kill me? A priest? You'll rot in hell!" Lucian laughed.

"Then I guess I shall see you there." He smoothly snapped the neck of his enemy. Lucian's cross pendant slipped from his collar as his neck went slack in death.

"May God forgive us both."

It was only moments before several men quickly surrounded Ethan and the body. The muscular, cloaked figures said little as they gathered Lucian's corpse and made ready to leave the abbey. Two of the men were mouthing rhythmic prayers and crossing themselves. Ethan could not readily see their faces, but each one bore a distinctive opal ring upon their hand.

"You are Ethan, are you not?" Michael asked.

"Aye." He lifted his hand to show the ring of his grandfather.

"Welcome, brother. You have been initiated so soon?"

"Ummm, I guess you could call it that. I just wanted to stop him. He was trying to rape my sister," Ethan tried to explain.

"Come with us," Michael turned and walked away. The men disappeared into the wooded hills near the castle with Lucian's body. They built a rather large bon fire and proceeded with an odd ceremony. They removed Lucian's cross and laid it aside. They laid hands upon his body and prayed over this priest who had lost his way, long ago. They prayed for reconciliation. They prayed for mercy. Ethan was expected to touch the body too.

"You must let go of the anger now. The deed is done," Michael explained, "We hold no grudges. We keep no records of past wrongs. We see it, we deal with it, and we move on. It is the way of the 33."

"How do you forgive?"

"We give it to God. 'Vengeance is mine, sayeth the Lord.'" Michael crossed himself. One of the priests beheaded Lucian and they burnt the body. When the ashes cooled, they placed them in a dark, carved box with velvet lining. They placed his head and his pendant on top of the ashes and sealed the box with the mark of the 33.

"Go home, my brother. We make ready to ride," Michael said as he began leading Ethan out of the forest.

"Where are you going? Shouldn't I be going as well?"

"You accomplished your task. It is up to us now. Go home and give your sister a hug. You will be hearing from us. When we need you, you will know it. Until then, be at peace, my friend. You have another path to follow just now. Follow your heart and we will never be far away." As Ethan made his way back to his parent's home, he caught a glimpse of a company of riders heading north toward the horizon. A few days later, Bishop Kincaid awoke to find the box resting on his doorstep.

CHAPTER 19

❀

PATHS

Janvier, 1310

Dalibar and the travelers prepared to be on their way several days after the wedding. No one knew what happened to Michalassi, but Dalibar was not heartbroken that the man would not be joining their journey. He didn't care for the way the troubadour eyed the women. They gathered in the great hall for one last warm meal before leaving Sedgemoor.

"If you are ever in need, my friend, you can come here," Tormond offered over a tankard of ale.

"I am in you debt, sir."

"Not at all. The music made the wedding and Christmas quite festive," the Laird smiled.

Father Bryan had been invited to join the family meal. He sat quietly, enjoying all that was going on around him. The recent tests of his faith, in both man and God, had done nothing to dampen his gentle nature. In trying times, he found that faith is either melted away, or it is turned to steel.

"I hope you are not planning to leave us as well, Father," Elspeth asked.

"Nay, m'lady. I should like to stay and serve you, if it is in your pleasure that I do so."

"I was afraid you would want to revoke your vows after what your teacher put you through."

"It was a test of faith, I admit. But in my heart, I feel there is still much good in the Church and my place in it. I still hear the call. Mayhap, I can bring about healing, where Lucian wrought havoc. If I walk away, then the enemy won. As long as I have breath, I won't let darkness win."

Ethan had been nervous all morning. He had spoken with his father into the wee hours about the future. He made Rod aware of all that had transpired with the 33 and Lucian's body. They discussed his future; his dreams of becoming a navigator like his hero, St. Brendan, and his feelings for Belinda. Rod could tell his boy was itching to stretch his wings. Ethan paced the great hall like a caged cat until he could bear it no longer.

"I have a bit of news," he began. All eyes, including Belinda's were on him.

"If it meets with Dalibar's approval, I shall be leaving with the travelers."

"My son is running away with the gypsies?" Jolie gasped, "Oh, no offense."

"None taken, dear lady," Dalibar nodded, "Why do you wish to journey with us? You are held in high esteem here. You have no idea how the world treats misplaced poets such as ourselves."

"Yes, I do. And if Belinda insists on going with you, then I must accompany her."

"Ah, a matter of the heart," the gypsy smiled, "Never let it be said that I am against love."

"You cannot be serious," Jolie whispered. Rod hugged her and kissed her cheek. "Nay, I agreed to let *one* of my boys go, not both of them on the same day! A peck on the cheek will not make things better, Rod!"

"Now, darlin'…"

"God's teeth, how I hate it when you try to pacify me!" she spat.

"Mother, can you not see that I am grown? I am a man, to all it seems, except you. Allow me to grow up, mother. You've raised me well. You've taught me faith, and honesty and hope. You taught me to dream, now let me live those dreams. I want your blessing," Ethan knelt before her. The hall was quiet as they watched Jolie. She placed a trembling hand upon the unruly brown curls of her son's head. She closed her eyes and took a deep breath. The time had come.

"Bless my son, Lord, indeed in all his ways. Let him bring glory to You in all he does. Let him be true to the path You have already laid out for him. Keep him far from evil, and surround him with love, amen," she sobbed. Ethan stood and took her in his arms. This small woman who had sculpted his life from the beginning, had just given him wings to fly.

"Thank you, mother," he whispered in her ear and placed a soft kiss there. He received a gruff hug from his father and a slap on the back from Ruffian, as the hall erupted in laughter and applause.

"Are we now even, sir knight?" Tessa nudged Ethan; "I have done all I can to secure your place with the fair Belinda. If you botch it up now, 'twill be on your head alone."

"Aye, m'lady, we are even. Keep my tooth as a personal gift; a little piece of myself," he smiled.

Before they left the castle, Tormond made sure that they were duly loaded with warm woolens and ample food for the journey. Ethan packed light, but brought along his tattered journals, his leather bound copy of *Navigatio Brendani*, in Italian, and his spyglass from Artemis.

"Here, 'tis about time you had a new one," Jolie handed him a new journal and quill, "You do remember the recipe for ink, do you not?"

"Aye mother, you have taught me well," he grinned.

"Go with God." She held him until he pried himself from her.

Ruffian and Tessa were snugly settled in one of the La Quesnay carriages. Lachlan and Thunder were ridden to Quesnay castle by Ruffian's men. The travelers accompanied the LaQuesnays, until the road diverged west. It would be the last time they would see Ethan for the next two years. As the group pulled out of Sedgemoor's gate, the MacLures and Bardougnes lifted their children up to God. A new horizon dawned bright and beautiful before them.

EPILOGUE

❀

A NEW DAY

Octobre', 1310
Quesnay castle

She lay there in blissful slumber. Her dreams were of far away places known only in her spirit. It had been a long night for Ruffian. He lay beside her, gazing at his bride in wonderment and awe.

The babes squirmed at her breast; a boy and girl both, coming into the world only moments apart. Dominic was bigger, but was gentle in spirit. Jewel, on the other hand, let out a lusty wail that woke her mother immediately. *Hmmm, I wonder where she gets that?* He grinned at the thought.

"Have you slept, husband?" she yawned.

"I'll sleep on the morrow," he said, "There is too much going on right now and I do not wish to miss anything."

"I'll wager that before we are done, you will have had more than your fill of crying babes and dirty drawers," she laughed.

"Nay, love, never," he whispered and kissed her softly.

He stepped over to his writing desk and gazed out their chamber window. Reaching for his quill, he scrolled in bold, sweeping lines, their family entries into the Bible.

All we can do is offer up those we love into His safekeeping. People and things are ours, only to be cherished for a little while, ultimately all creation belongs to the Creator. The most precious gift is the realization that life is fleeting. It is at that moment, we truly begin to live each day, treasuring those God has given us.

Treasure those around you.
I bid Thee Peace ~

THE HOUSE OF La QUESNAY

❁

Dominic Rene La Quesnay   married   Marguerite Aimee Bouchard

Their Children:

Adrian Dominic,   Aimee Renee,   Reginald Paul

Adrian Dominic La Quesnay   married   Journey deau Jourdaine

Their Children:

Jordan   Rapheal

Rapheal La Quesnay   married   Contessa Faith MacLure

Their Children:

Dominic Tormond La Quesnay   Jewel deau Faith La Quesnay

THE HOUSE OF CELESTINE/ESSEX

❀

Theobold Essex married Madelynn Celestine*

Their son:
William Essex married Margaret Bell

Their daughter:
Elspeth Essex married Tormond MacLure

William Essex (2nd marriage) to Celeste Augerine

Their daughter:
Jolie Celeste Essex married Roderick Bardougne

Children of Elspeth Essex and Tormond MacLure:

Leland Contessa Faith

Leland MacLure married Hope McKinnon

Contessa Faith MacLure married Rapheal La Quesnay

Children of Jolie Essex and Roderick Bardougne:

Rapheal LaQuesnay, Ethan Roderick, Serrah Celeste

HOUSE OF MACLURE

❀

Leod   married   Mary of Crotach

Their children:

Rory MacLeod   Leland MacLeod   John MacLeod   Derrick MacLeod
m. Megan of Lewis   (died)   m. Camilla Bolthby   m. Kathryn Daniels

Alisdare MacLure   William of Crotach   1. Donald MacLure
m. Brigid of Skye   2. Norman of Leod

Tormond Alisdare MacLure
   b.1264
m. Elspeth Essex

1. Leland MacLure
m. Hope McKinnon

2. Contessa Faith MacLure
m. Rapheal LaQuesnay

SECRETS OF THE 33

From the vestiges of time, they have come.
Some say from Brendan himself, they came,
A priest from the land of Eryn,
With visions for the future,
Of sailing the world,
Of laying a foundation of faith in the Lord of all.

The brotherhood was built upon
The blood of those who came before,
Those that died for their faith;
For their God,
In the face of a cruel world.

Their number is few ~ only 33.
The 3 of the blessed Trinity,
33 years the Lord walked the earth on His mission.
The mission remains ~
To lead people to the cross,
To show them the Savior,
High and lifted up.
Glorified.

They are born into this destiny.
But they are not made aware ~
Until it is their time and place to serve.

They retire only by death.
The cycle never ceases.

Though priests, they are also men;
Warriors.
They will fight to the death to preserve and protect
That which God has ordained.
They are the remnant, all that still remain of a faithful people,
Whose only desire was to serve the Lord and glorify Him
By the blessing of others in an unforgiving land.

Though priests, they are also men;
Some, husbands and fathers.
Their offspring is the seed that ensures
The continuation of the mission.
They love and laugh,
They are the embodiment of strength,
And knowledge,
And passion.

Though they are priests, they are also men;
Messengers who roam the land with wisdom.
They are in the shadows; they wait.
They guard. They protect.

They will take a life in a twinkling of an eye, if need be.
They will never hesitate to end evil.
The vengeance is swift, and sure.

They are the remnant.
All that remains of a faithful few.
And I ~
I am the scribe who records the living history,
As it unfolds.

0-595-27425-0